THE SECRET WITHIN

SEAN PLATT

DAVID W. WRIGHT

STERLING & STONE

For Anna

THE SECRET WITHIN

ONE

Anika

"You fucking bitch!"

Anika hurls herself into the bathroom, slams the door, heart racing, panting, fear clenching her chest.

He bangs. "Open the fucking door!"

"I didn't mean to, I swear."

"Open the fucking door, Anika, or else!"

She hears him pacing.

He's going to hurt her again. And this time, who knows how bad it will be.

Anika wonders how the hell she got here. Why couldn't she ever catch a break? From one abusive house to another as a child, from stuck in the foster system to right now at this moment in her miserable life.

She finally found a good family, and thought she had turned her life around. But bad luck acted like it was her best friend and always caught up with her.

"Open the fucking door, Anika!" Jay screams, back to his pounding.

Why hasn't anyone heard him? Or intervened? It's a nice apartment building, the kind that doesn't bury its collective head when someone is screaming and wrecking a place.

"Open the fucking door, open the fucking door, open the fucking door!"

Anika wishes she'd thought to bring the phone with her, but she isn't sure where she left it.

Everything happened so fast.

She can lie. He probably doesn't know where her phone is. "Go away. I'm gonna call the cops."

Jay stops.

And for a moment she thinks he bought her lie.

Then he laughs.

"Your phone is out here, you dumb cunt. Open the door or I swear to God I'll fucking kill you."

She prays, but God isn't there, and Anika's call goes to someone else.

TWO

Delaney

I wake to a call on my business line.

"Delaney West," I say, trying to clear the sleep from my head as I sit up in bed.

"You're the private investigator who found that missing Kolchev girl last year, right?"

"How can I help you?"

I'm hoping this isn't a call for another missing child. Those cases often end badly, much as I enjoy the rare occasions when they don't. They're usually evidence that my psychic "gift" is a curse in too many ways.

"My name is Marsha Sutherland and I need you to find my child. The police have given up."

Fuck.

I grab the notepad and pen from my nightstand and flip to a clean page.

"Excuse me ... are you there?"

"Tell me about it," I say.

My cat, Pumpkin, hops his oversized orange tabby ass up on my bed and gives me the usual look: *Feed me.*

I pet his head and he hisses like an asshole.

"His name is Jay Sutherland," Marsha answers, then pauses, as if I might recognize the name.

"How old is he?"

"Twenty-three."

"So, he's not a missing *child*."

"No, but he is *my child*. And he's missing. The police aren't doing a damn thing."

"How long has he been missing?"

"Three months."

I ask all the usual questions, trying to determine if her son is truly missing or just didn't want anything to do with his family. Parents *think* they know their kids, but it's often an illusion — either self-perpetuated or one their child wants them to see.

As a cop, I've stood next to way too many grieving parents, stunned to find their adult offspring overdosed in a seedy hotel, or one of several bodies in a shootout between rival gangs, or in a murder suicide.

Occasionally I could tell that the parents knew in their deepest heart that this was where their child would end up. Usually, they seemed genuinely surprised. I always wondered the same thing — *when did they stop seeing their child?*

Had their blindness led to their kid's destiny?

How culpable were they?

And what the hell were they doing that they felt was more important than raising their children?

Mrs. Sutherland is frustrated, like she's been through this a hundred times. Probably has been. I ask if she's hired other PIs. She hasn't, and for reasons she doesn't seem too keen on discussing. Something's off about her, and my instincts are screaming at me, practically demanding that I run the other way.

But my bills don't pay themselves. And I hate to write anybody off based on a phone call.

I arrange a meeting. I prefer not to meet clients at my office, because I'm working out of my tiny apartment right now, and I don't want people in my place.

Thankfully, she asks me over to her house.

TWO HOURS later and I'm pulling up to the Sutherland house, a palatial residence cresting a knoll in the prestigious gated community of Arbor Falls.

I did a little research before I left so I know who I'm dealing with. Troy is a former B-List actor turned internet marketing "success coach," whatever the fuck that is. His freely available videos are all of him speaking platitudes and flexing his wealth. Shot in one of his expensive sports cars, on his boat, or onstage speaking to sheep, similar in their way to those that believed in my father for so long.

For $5997, you too can be an internet marketing douchebag!

The man is an obvious huckster.

Marsha isn't much better, hawking her essential (snake) oils and overpriced "natural medicines" as a health guru. A faux hippy conning folks who don't know better, preaching anti-medicine bullshit that borders on hazardous if one were to take her advice.

And their missing son, from what I've seen on social media, seems like a typical college jock asshole. Friends called him "Big Jay" and some additional research tells me he played one year as a quarterback, a good one from what I could see, before getting accused of rape.

The case was dropped, the girl probably paid off, but the kid lost his scholarship. Every photo and video on Jay's feed is him hanging with his boys, getting drunk or high or flaunting his "hoes." It always surprises me how often people get accused of terrible shit, then still leave incriminating photos and video like stains across their channels. But kids like this one, who never had to face any genuine consequences, rarely think shit through.

Despite me not liking any of these people from what I've seen, there's still a missing person. Even dickbags don't deserve the misery of wondering whether their child is dead.

I ring the bell and wait three beats before Marsha opens the door.

She's blonde and even prettier than in her videos, though her nose has seen a few too many scalpels and her skin is splotchy from tanning. She's wearing all white, except for a sapphire scarf at her neck.

"Thank you for coming," she says.

I'm uncomfortable with hugs, especially from strangers, but I swallow my distaste. Her embrace is slight and our skin doesn't touch, so I'm not bombarded with this woman's emotions.

I don't need my abilities to figure her out. I can read her fine. She's reserved, surrounding herself with a wealthy lifestyle to steer clear of her internal needs. She's unhappy but hides it behind her bubbly, hippie persona. She's probably stuck in a miserable marriage but admitting that means confessing to a procession of wrong choices. Sometimes people believe it's better to stick it out or plow through. Admitting you're wrong means starting over and reinventing yourself. There are few things harder than that.

"Good to meet you."

"Troy is on a call. He'll be right with us." She leads me into the living room. The house is practically a mansion, yet still somehow cozy in earth tones and subtle brush-strokes gracing the ample canvases that pepper the walls. The air smells of citrus and rosemary. Probably one of the essential blends Marsha hawks on her site.

We sit catty-corner from each other on matching lush leather sofas with a finely-crafted oak coffee table. It looks more like an art installation than a piece of functional furniture.

She hands me a professional-looking headshot of her son, smiling and sober. Dressed in a Sunday tie. Nothing like his LiveLyfe posts. "This is Jay. He was a quarterback two years ago at Oregon State before his injury."

What injury, his reputation? So she's not even gonna tell me the truth?

I resist calling her on it. Not a great way to start if they want me to find their son. I need to know what kind of person he really is.

"Tell me when's the last time you saw Jay."

"I'd rather wait until Troy is here." Marsha stands. "Can I get you anything to drink?"

"No, thanks. I'm good."

She heads to the kitchen, takes a moment, probably pausing to give her husband more time, then returns with a glass of red wine.

Troy enters from another room, slipping his phone into his pocket as he crosses the threshold. His smile is immediate and insincere. "Hello, Ms. West, glad to meet you."

I take his hand and get a rush of emotions — anger, greed, and lust. Skepticism, too. A flash of him fucking a young Asian woman in knee-high socks.

The more secrets someone has, the more strongly their touch will broadcast emotion. The body isn't designed to lie. The truth always comes out. It can bleed through their actions or it can come from me picking up on their errant emotions. Troy Sutherland's scream from his pores. If I held his hand long enough, I'd get deeper glimpses into his darkness, whether I wanted them or not.

My father called my touch a gift from God. It's helped me do my job and put some bad people away, even find or save a few good ones, but I can never turn it off. So even the silence for me is a detuned radio, screaming in my ear and threatening my sanity.

I do my best to mask my discomfort, plastering my fake smile on as I pump Troy's hand and release. Resist the urge to wipe my hand on my jeans, then take my seat as he sits beside his wife on the other couch.

"So, how did you *really* find that missing Russian girl? Was it, as the news said, a *psychic* thing, or good old-fashioned detective work?"

His smile is so smug I want to crack it.

Marsha purses her lips.

I return his counterfeit smile.

I'm used to skepticism. Hell, I'm dubious of all those damned people peddling their services as a psychic — especially those offering to reveal the future for coin.

"I think what you're really asking is whether I'm truly a psychic. Is that right, Mr. Sutherland?"

His smile falters. "Forgive me, I guess I'm a bit of a cynic. Lots of frauds in my line of work."

"People selling hope to desperate people. Damned parasites, am I right?" I resist the urge to wink. "But I didn't take the case to get paid. I took it as a personal favor to someone."

"Yes, but you *did* get a lot of free publicity, am I right?" He sits back, arms folded in his lap. I half-expect him to say *Gotcha.*

"But she *did* find the girl, right?" Marsha looks at me, a painful hope in her eyes taking me back to all those people in my father's church, looking for me to save them.

She's the only reason I haven't gotten up and left — yet.

"I found the girl because I saw the darkness left behind. It led me from her bedroom to the place she was being held."

It's a simplification of a more complex sequence of events, but close enough.

"What do you mean … *darkness?*" I'm not sure if Troy is still challenging me or if he's turned genuinely curious. Annoyance clouds my thinking.

"Have you ever walked into a place that felt off? You weren't sure why, but something about it was definitely wrong?"

Marsha nods. Troy continues to observe me. A salesman waiting for the pitch, looking for the hidden tricks to either recognize or adopt for himself.

"When bad things happen, it leaves a sort of stain, or an echo behind. Most people feel it even if they don't know how to identify it."

Troy finally says, "But you … *you* can identify it."

"Yes."

He stares at me for a long moment.

Marsha clears her throat and waits for me to look her way.

"Jay vanished three months ago. The police won't do anything because he's been in trouble with the law ever since … an incident at school. They accuse him of all sorts of things. He's no angel, but our son certainly isn't the devil."

"What sorts of things?" I ask.

Troy answers. "They asked about his affiliation with this drug dealer, said that he owed some people money. But hell if they ever arrested the drug dealer or anything. Our taxes cover these clowns' salaries and they can't even do their damned jobs."

"Do you suspect that this drug dealer killed him?" I ask. "Maybe some sort of retribution?"

Marsha blows her nose in what's left of the napkin, starting to sob. "I don't think he's dead."

"What did the police say? You filed a missing person's report, right?"

Troy says, "Yes, but they're saying he took this dealer's drugs and split."

"He would never do that. Not our Jay."

"Did he use drugs?"

Marsha swallows, then gets defensive. "Show me a college kid who doesn't experiment."

I meet her eyes and calmly say, "I'm not looking to accuse Jay of anything, but I need to know everything you know to find out what happened."

"Can you find him?" The hope is back in her eyes.

"I don't know yet. But I'll do everything I can."

Troy clears his throat, stands, grabs a glass of wine for himself, then takes a sip before asking, "And how much would this cost?"

I give him an estimate.

"No guarantees?"

"I'd be lying if I guaranteed anything, Mr. Sutherland."

"But you're a psychic. Don't you just know?" Troy smiles like he planted a flag in that joke.

"It doesn't work like that."

"Why work at all? If you're psychic, why not win the lottery and retire, Ms. Jennings?"

Jennings.

Shit.

"See, I'm just wondering why the famous Delaney West, daughter of the infamous pastor Ted Jennings, would change her name. Wouldn't she be *proud* of her family legacy?"

Marsha seems surprised by this turn of events. "What's going on, Troy?"

"What's going on is that you hired a fraud psychic to look for our son. Daughter of that pastor that conned all those people out of money before getting sent off to jail. I went against my better judgment and allowed you to call her, but … my gut says not to trust this woman. Why don't you ask her about the scam she and her daddy ran on people for years."

Marsha stares at me as I stand.

"Where you going?" Troy gets up and moves toward me as if he intends to block my exit. "Go ahead, tell my wife all about you and your old man, ripping off the sick and elderly, claiming to heal them."

I meet his eyes, then turn to Marsha. She looks confused, and I feel bad for her, but I'm not arguing about something I've worked hard to put behind me. And I'm certainly not bowing down for this woman's asshole husband.

"I wish you luck in finding your son."

I turn to leave.

Troy leans in to bump me, just enough to let me feel the strength of a big strong man.

I stumble back.

My eyes seize on his weakest points, his eyes, his neck closest to me. I could take him out at the knees. It would be delicious to wipe that smug look from his face, and I wouldn't need but a second to do it.

I leave, before my anger gets the better of me.

I climb into my car, pound the steering wheel and scream, "Fuck!"

I tear out of there, eager to put as much distance between myself, that man, and my past as possible.

THREE

Anika

Anika stands in the restroom stall waiting for her panic to subside.

One moment she was grabbing lettuce from the walk-in, and the next her chest was tight, a certainty that something awful was about to happen.

She'd fled the kitchen, went to the bathroom, and puked.

Now she's standing in the stall, staring down at her sickness still floating in the toilet.

She flushes the mess, leaves the stall, and goes to the sink and rinses her mouth out with water.

It would be so much easier if she still had painkillers, but she'd flushed them a week after Jay's disappearance. She'd been clean for nearly ninety days since.

You are fine.

Nothing is wrong.

Just head back out there before Jerry starts whining that his drink is empty.

Anika leaves the restroom to find the hostess, Jolene,

seating a table of twelve for dinner in Candi (*with an i*)'s station, despite the fact that it's Anika's turn.

What the hell?

It's already a slow day at Paddy's Ale House, and Candi has three tables to Anika's one. Salt in the wound, the party is full of well-dressed men and women, coworkers from the looks of things. That means drinks on a Friday, followed by a big fat tip.

It should be my table.

YES, IT SHOULD.

The voice Anika's heard since she was a child is a comfort like always. The part of her she always turns to when stressed. A voice to advise her through the worst of things.

While Jolene is seating the large party, Anika walks past the hostess stand trying not to be obvious, and checks the chart for an R next to Candi's name, wanting to see if there's a legitimate request from the group.

But of course there's not, which means that Jolene screwed her yet again.

Anika considers saying something, but she doesn't have the seniority, and clearly Jolene doesn't like her. Candi and Jolene are roommates, so Candi always gets the best guests and big tippers while Anika gets stuck with the groups of obnoxious teens, or the regulars nobody else wants because they're difficult, camp at their table all afternoon, or tip like shit.

As if God decided to remind Anika just how shitty her day, week, month, and year are all going, her only table is a regular nobody likes yet she somehow inherited. A lecherous fat man named Jerry, who could barely contain his creepy arousal when ogling the female servers. Despite his antiquity, the old man seemed particularly into petite, young-looking girls, like Anika.

He raises his hand and whistles.

She hates when customers whistle to get her attention. Even more so when it's Jerry.

She plasters on a fake smile and approaches his table.

"Hey, sweetie, get me another Coke, would you?"

Anika takes his cup that's sticky with God only knows what food residue and swaps it for a clean one. Fills it with ice and Coke, then returns to his table.

"Could you also get me more napkins?"

She resists her sigh, then brings him new napkins.

Only then does Jerry ask if she'd *also* get him some more mayo packs, even though he's almost done with his sandwich. He's just going to shove them into his over-stuffed denim fanny pack with a giant flag on the front and take them home like always. A terrible tipper, who sees the restaurant's condiments as his personal resupply for home.

Anika hates him, but brings him one mayo pack and sets it on the table anyway.

He stares at it, his eyebrows arched. "One pack? Come on, hon, don't be stingy."

Taking him to task will only cost her his tip, which will be thirteen percent at most. Plus, he'll probably complain to her manager, Ken.

Jerry is a lecherous cheap bastard, but he eats here twice a day. With the newer, nicer diners down the road, Ken does everything possible to keep his regulars happy.

"Oh, I'm sorry. That was the last one. I didn't want you to wait while I found another box to open. I'll go and grab you some more."

His eyebrows settle and he says, "No problem."

Anika walks away from him venting a tiny sigh this time, almost hoping he'll hear it. Sometimes passive-aggressive is her best route through the day.

After handing Jerry his stupid mayo, Anika busies

herself restocking the ketchup, salt, and pepper bottles at her tables while waiting for Jerry to finally leave.

"See ya next time, sweetie." He rakes her with his gaze as he passes.

She dresses conservatively, with a collared black polo and jeans. Candi's in a tight top and bootie shorts, but Anika still feels naked when Jerry looks her way. She wishes the dark restaurant was even darker so she could slip into the shadows and escape his gaze.

"Bye, Jerry," she says, making her way over to clean his mess and collect her whopping thirteen percent, at most.

Three hours into her shift and Anika hasn't earned close to minimum wage. Days like this make her wish she'd chosen any other profession. She'd been through a lot these last few years. It was hard to focus on going to school or keeping a steady job, so she resorted to one of the few where she could still make decent money despite her limited resources. The plan just isn't panning out at Paddy's.

She watches Candi work the table of twelve, flirting with a few of the men, and the women, to maximize her tip.

Anika's section is still crickets.

Paddy's used to be a hot spot, or at least that's what Anika had heard from Ken, an awkward thirty-six-year-old balding man with a beer gut who often tries to impress her by declaring the importance of both him and his restaurant. It has the ambiance of a chain, but with enough local flavor and personalization to feel like it breaks from the franchise pack. Necessary in a city like Barton. They like things that are old and run down, same as they like them gleaming and new. So the city is a honkytonk metropolis with plenty of both. Paddy's always does well in-season, but the off-season is killing them more by the year.

Packed, the place feels modern and fun. Empty it feels like an antiquated has-been whose time has long since passed it by. A sad leftover from another era. Ironically hip during better times, now kitschy and lame. An echo in earnest.

Paddy's feels like the guy at the party laughing along with a joke until he realizes in one sickening epiphany that *he* is what everyone's laughing at.

In addition to the area's two new restaurants, Barton's downtown is undergoing lots of construction. That makes Paddy's even harder to reach and unworthy of the hassle for most patrons. Fortunately, at peak times, those other restaurants are harder to get in as well, so in addition to its regulars, Paddy's ends up with the overflow, occasional work party or "girls' night out."

Anika hopes it will get busier before Caite and Brian come in at six. If business doesn't pick up, she'll be the first to get cut.

And the last thing she wants is to go home.

She needs to occupy herself, especially at night, when the urge to use is strongest.

Anika could call Chelsea, her foster sister and the closest thing she has to family. Anika hasn't seen her in some time. Married with a little girl, and finally happy. She doesn't want to bring her sister down or worry her, so Anika hasn't been returning her calls. She also doesn't want Chelsea to know what she's been up to, because Anika always feels as though her sister is looking down on her.

But she misses Chelsea, especially now, and decides to call her later. She's clean, so Anika won't feel as guilty being around Chelsea and her little girl.

She busies herself cleaning tables, even though they're immaculate, making sure to look busy so Ken, who peeks out from the back every so often, will see that *she* is being productive while Candi and Jolene spend downtime on their phones, like they both are now.

Anika looks up to see two parties coming in — one a group of six professional women in their thirties and forties, and the other a thin, short man wearing a blue hoodie, face covered, entering just behind them.

The six-top should go to Anika. But Jolene proceeds to lead them over to Candi's table.

What the hell?

She sits the loner dude at one of Anika's many empty booths.

Anika has had enough.

She approaches Jolene at the podium, and takes a look to double check that there's no R next to the table she just sat.

"Why didn't you sit the women with me? *I* was up."

Jolene looks at Anika like she's being petty. "They always sit with Candi."

"Did they request her? I didn't see an R."

"They don't need to request, they're her regulars."

Anika wants to scream.

Jolene is staring at her with that stupid expression, her big vacant blue eyes beneath horribly short-cropped bangs.

"This is the second big table you've given her when I was up. I want the next big group, whether I'm up or not."

"Whatever." Jolene rolls her eyes. "You gonna get your customer's order or sit here whining all day?"

Anika huffs away, and goes to her only customer.

He pulls his hoodie back as she approaches, revealing a familiar face.

"Long time no see, stranger."

FOUR

Delaney (Age 7)

I'm seven years old, frightened back in church's rear room.

Father crouches in front of me with a coaxing smile. "Come on, Del. Just one tonight. Then you can rest until the weekend."

"I'm tired," I plead.

It's late and a school night. Even though I'm home-schooled, my instructor arrives promptly at 7:30 a.m. every weekday. Inga has no patience for sleepy kids.

I want to go home and crawl into bed with a book.

"Please, honey. A lot of people paid good money to see you do your thing."

I want to explain how much my stomach hurts, but Father always dismisses it as childish laziness, me trying to resist my "true calling." He says I owe it to his parishioners, and God Himself, to do what I was born to do.

"I don't want to do *my thing*. I want to be a normal kid, not a freak show."

He smacks me hard across the face.

"Where'd you hear that … *freak show?*"

I don't want to tell him that I've overheard kids in his

congregation whispering the phrase while laughing about me.

I tremble, my tears welling.

"Don't you dare cry," Father snaps, hands gripping both of my shoulders as his blue eyes drill into mine. I've been told that mine are pretty and blue, but his are anything but. They're dark and scary, almost cobalt. They look *through* more than *at* me, off to someplace only he can see.

"We don't have time for this silliness. You have a job to do, young lady. And you're going to march right out there and do it. Do you understand me?"

What else can I say?

"Yes, sir."

"Good." As much as I fear him, Father's smile still always makes me feel safe and loved.

He hugs me.

I STAND BACKSTAGE, listening for my cue as Father, Mother in her prettiest blue dress, and Brother Clarence, my father's "right hand man," invite everyone in the room to witness the glory of God. A true miracle. His power and grace.

"Would you please welcome my daughter, and vessel of His Blessings, The Great Delaney."

Applause as the curtains part. The church is full to capacity, more than five hundred people, then even more standing outside in the cold night, all here to witness a miracle.

My stomach is still grumbling, but I throttle the fear, doing a thing Inga recently taught me — disconnecting myself, she called it.

I disconnect so the things are happening to my body while the Real Me, my soul, hides inside. Safe and sound where nobody can hurt me.

My parents are standing before the congregation with Brother Clarence, everyone on their feet.

Father says something but his words are lost. I can't stop focusing on the faces staring back at me. I've done this eleven times, and the expressions keep getting scarier. It's not that I'm frightened by them. They don't want to hurt me. It's the hope in their eyes, that I might heal them or a loved one. But I can't help everyone and that scares me — letting so many of them down, people who desperately need me to cure them.

Father is still talking but nobody's looking at him. Every eye is on me, tears dripping into their open mouths. Some are reaching out, as if my touch alone might heal them.

But it won't.

I look at Mother. She smiles like she always does on stage. She saves her sorrow for home. I'm not sure why Mom cries so much. "It's grownup stuff," she said, the one time I felt brave enough to ask.

Father doesn't hit her, at least not that I know of. And they seem happy. She even leads a women's group to help couples suffering from marriage problems.

But something is wrong and I can see it, even through her smile.

She looks away as if she knows I see it and that scares her.

Father asks for tonight's special guest to come forth and receive his blessing.

I don't know who I'm healing. I never do until I start.

But tonight I recognize the man as someone who attended church a year ago, before he fell ill and became confined to a wheelchair. The town's mayor, Ed Brayhall.

I'm not sure what he has, some disease that people whisper about like the man is already dead. His body is twisted and his face is pained.

As Brother Clarence wheels him to the stage, toward Father and me, that feeling in my stomach gets even worse. Something is wrong. I don't know *how* I know, but I'm certain in the same way I can feel how to help these people. Everything's there in my head.

I can't look at him.

He's too sad looking. Like Mom, but scary.

I look at the ground.

My father's hand falls on my shoulder, prodding me to look up.

"Mayor Brayhall has suffered indignities that no man should suffer, that no man of God should be forced to endure. And still, he's never lost faith. Crippled and diseased in his prime, if any man should've lost his belief in Our Heavenly Father, Mayor Brayhall had reason. But his faith never wavered, and now it shall be rewarded by Christ through my child."

Father pauses, same as always before the next part. "Are you ready to witness His work through The Great Delaney?"

"Yes!" some say, while others chant, "Praise be," or some other words of worship directed at God, and me because they think that He is working through me.

I don't think it's God. Not that I could ever tell Father.

I look up and meet the crowd's gaze because that's what I'm supposed to do. I smile like I'm told.

"Delaney, are you ready to deliver the Lord's blessings unto this wretched man?"

"Yes, Father."

The crowd roars.

"Are you ready to show us all the power of faith in Our Lord Jesus Christ?"

"Yes, Father."

The crowd roars even louder.

"Then heal this man!"

He takes my hands and leads me to Mayor Brayhall.

He's paralyzed from the waist down, his body a curled, cruel comma withering away in the wheelchair. Gnarled hands on his lap, twisted in ways that hands should not twist.

His sunken eyes move up to meet mine. This man is not looking at me as others have before him. There is no awe or hope for a cure.

There's something else in his gaze.

Something I don't have a name for.

Rotten and terrifying.

Father takes my hands and puts them on the man's.

In an instant, everybody is gone.

The world around us is dark. There is only me and the mayor in his chair.

But there's someone else, too.

Someone or something inside the mayor, watching me with its icy black eyes.

"Hello, child," says its sick voice in my head. *"We meet at last."*

FIVE

Delaney

What the actual fuck?

I open my eyes to the back of Gerard's head. What the hell is he doing here?

I push him. I'm not sure if he's awake, but he turns in the bed and looks at me, eyebrows knotted in confusion.

"What are you doing?"

"What?" He's playing dumb.

"You're sleeping."

"Yeah, it's late."

I get out of bed, pissed. "You know the rules. No sleeping over."

"Oh, come on, Del. How long do we have to date before I earn sleepover privileges?"

"How long have we been dating?"

"You don't know?"

"I'm asking, aren't I?"

"Eight months. Eight months exclusively, Del."

"Not long enough. Get up."

"What?"

I grab the comforter and pull it away, exposing his naked body.

He curls up, cold. "Are you serious?"

I look to the corner of the bed where Pumpkin is sitting, staring at him. If cats can scowl, then that's what he's giving Gerard. "Pumpkin, am I serious?"

The cat looks over at him, then dismissively away.

"See, even Pumpkin can't believe you'd pull this shit."

"*What shit?* I fell asleep. It's not some sinister plan to move in. Yes, I'll fall asleep and maybe she won't notice until I'm suddenly living here!"

I look him up and down. I can almost always tell when somebody is lying. It's a gift as much as it's a curse. My anger dissipates, but I still want him gone.

I grab his boxers and pants from the floor and toss them at him. "Come on. Chop chop, clock's ticking."

He looks like he's going to protest further, but then starts getting dressed. He sighs as he stands. I'm not sure why, but I love when my pretty boy sighs in frustration. Makes me want to mess with him.

"You need to get back into therapy."

"Duly noted," I say, leading him into my tiny living room, grabbing his wallet, phone, and holstered gun before handing them all over.

"Seriously, Del. This ain't right. I've never dated anyone who was so weird about me staying over."

"You're absolutely right. You *have* never dated anyone like me."

"You're more like a lot of dudes I know than any girl I've dated."

"If I'm a dude, does that make *you* the girl?" I reach out and curl my fingers through his curtain of hair. He hates when I call him pretty boy. His work buddies bust his balls about the same thing. There are worse things to be razzed about.

"Should I call you Geraldine? Or maybe Gertrude?"

Another sigh.

I want to giggle, but I'm trying to maintain a serious expression so he doesn't know I'm not pissed that he fell asleep. Rules are rules and I take them seriously, even if he didn't mean anything by it.

"You're okay dating me. Hell, you were okay fucking me the night we met, but eight months later and I still can't stay over?"

"Should I call Pumpkin in to answer that?"

Gerard shakes his head. He barely tolerates my cat. And my cat can't stand him. Then again, my cat hates everyone, including me. But whatever, at least cats aren't needy bitches.

"Seriously. How long until you trust me enough to sleep over, or stay at my place?"

"I don't know."

Another sigh, and this time I feel bad. He thinks I don't let him sleep over because of my trust issues, or some other thing I've blamed it on before. Sure, I *do* have some serious trust issues, but I can't tell Gerard the real reason I don't do sleepovers. Or anybody else.

"How long do you expect us to go on like this?" He's suddenly too serious for my mood.

"I—"

"—don't know?" he finishes, his jaw firm.

I hate hurting him, but I hate him pushing me even more. We've talked about this too many times before.

"If you can't accept me as I am, there are other women out there, Gerard. No need to waste your time on me."

I don't mean for that to sound like a guilt trip, or that I

don't care about him. My relationships are doomed. I can't be with someone long-term for the same reason I don't do sleepovers. I should end things before I hurt him for good.

He stares at me. Then, a bit too pouty he says, "I guess I know where I stand."

He probably wants me to apologize or stop him from going. But I say nothing as he shuts the door, just short of a slam. He wouldn't be the first.

I let out a sigh, annoyed.

I do like Gerard, and I'm comfortable with him. I'm also not ready to find a replacement guy to keep me from boredom. It's too much work, and there are too many flaky men out there. Too possessive and alpha or too needy and beta. Gerard sits nicely in the middle. An interesting guy. Into scary movies like me, and a detective — the job I almost went for before going the PI route. So we talk lots of shop and rant about idiots. He's fun to talk to and hang out with. A safe bet, I thought, since he wasn't looking for something serious.

But they all say that.

None of them are looking for anything serious until they realize they can't have me. Then the relationship feels like an exercise in sobriety.

I head to the fridge, grab an ice cold beer, crack off the cap, and take a long swallow. I sit at my desk and open my laptop, thinking of working before getting discouraged at the sight of a stack of unpaid bills awaiting my attention.

Fuck this.

I close the laptop and stand.

Ten minutes later, I'm sitting in the hot tub outside, listening to the pleasant sounds of bubbling water while staring up at what I can see of the night sky on the other side of a thick cloud of light pollution.

I like the pool area at night. I come here a lot when I

can't sleep, or wake from nightmares. I'd come during the day, but it's almost always packed with the other tenants. And even when it's not, the noisy teens are usually around to ruin things.

Footsteps approaching, along with the sound of a metal collar and claws padding toward me — my next-door neighbor's Chihuahua Jack Russel mix.

"Hey, Brandy," I say, scratching the happy dog under her chin.

Her tail starts wagging as her owner, Sebastian, carrying a beer of his own — non-alcoholic like always — approaches in his work uniform, dark blue EMT overalls. A tall, handsome black man in his mid-thirties with a strong jaw and kind green eyes. Seb would be my type, if he were into women. There's something about him that's different from everyone else I know. Nothing I can define or explain. An odd psychic smell, or at least that's the best I can explain it.

"Just getting home?" I ask.

"Ten minutes ago. Saw Gerard leaving in a huff. You all okay?"

"Just the usual. He tried to sleep over."

"Ah," Seb says, taking a swig of his beer. "And?"

"Pumpkin said no bueno."

"*Pumpkin.* Of course. Not *you.*"

I smile. "How's Ned?"

"He's passed out."

"He okay?" I ask.

Seb's husband recently hurt his back while rearranging his art studio.

"Still in some pain, but he'll be okay. Stubborn bastard was trying to move stuff again."

"What?"

"Yeah, you and he are both stubborn bastards."

"I'm not stubborn, I'm *set in my ways*. Just like Ned," I tease as Brandy runs over to the bushes at the pool's border to pee.

"Yeah, well, he's fifty-five. *He* has an excuse. You're too young for that much obstinance."

"How old do you think I am?"

He shakes his head. "My mama always told me never ask a woman her age."

"You're guessing, not asking."

"Even worse!"

"Go ahead. I'm not hung up on that shit."

"Um, thirty-two?"

"What? I'm twenty-four, you bastard!"

"Oh my God, I'm *sooooo* sorry." Seb raises his hands, palms out.

"Nah, I'm just fucking with you, I'm thirty-two."

"You're such a bitch, Del."

"Thank you. At least I've got my youthful looks, eh?"

Brandy pads back over and plops on the ground beside me, belly out. I pet her as she squirms. I can't imagine Pumpkin *ever* letting me pet his fluffy white belly. Four seconds maybe, before he remembers to claw the shit out of my arm.

Seb takes another drink, then tosses his near-beer into a nearby trashcan. He looks down at my bottle and I can tell he's thinking about asking for a sip. But he's six months sober, and I don't want to tempt him, so I finish it off and set the empty behind me.

There's an awkward moment of silence. I struggle to fill it, pretending to be more troubled about the Gerard situation than I am.

"Why does he want to sleep over so bad, anyway? You'd think most guys would welcome a girl that fucks them right then leaves them be."

"I dunno, maybe he *loves you* or something."

"That can't be it," I say, burping obnoxiously to earn myself a laugh.

"He's probably intoxicated by your feminine delicacy."

"Yes, that must be it."

"You've gotta let someone in, Del. Life's too long to go solo. Believe me."

"Nah, I'm good."

He shakes his head. "You don't want to be an old, lonely cat lady, do you?"

"You need multiple cats for that. Pumpkin won't let me have any more. And he's never going to die, so I'll probably never achieve true Cat Lady status."

"Seriously, you can't push everybody away."

"I don't push *everybody* away. I'm friends with you and Ned."

"We lived here for two years before you even said *hi*."

"I take my time warming up to people."

"I'll say."

"We're good friends now, right? It's not like I'm an ice queen."

"You do raise some serious walls."

"And they've served me well over the years. Have you *seen* the kinds of people out there?"

"Yeah, but you've never exactly struck me as timid. Remember that guy that harassed Ned and me at that restaurant?"

I laugh.

"Dude was twice the size of either of us and you decked him in the neck. *In the neck*, Del! Then you sat right back down and kept drinking, daring the guy to come back."

"He was a big pussy. And you're right, I'm not afraid. I

just don't have time for bullshit people or their bullshit problems. I've got enough going on with my father."

"How's he doing?"

I shake my head, wishing for another beer. "Don't wanna go there."

"Okay." Another long, awkward silence, then, "Is he the reason why you're …"

"I'm what?"

"Never mind."

"A lonely Cat Lady? No, I don't have daddy issues, if that's what you're asking. Maybe mommy issues. She's the one that left without saying a word."

"I didn't mean to pry."

"It's all good." I smile to let him know I'm fine. "Maybe in another few years I'll tell you why I'm such a damaged soul."

He smiles back, then picks up his dog. "Come on, girl, we've gotta get to bed. Early day tomorrow."

"Working in the morning?"

"No. Got to take Ned to the chiropractor."

"Ah, well, give Ned my best."

"Goodnight, Del."

"Goodnight, Brandy," I say, teasing Sebastian.

After a few minutes of silence, I head up to my place, planning to drink myself to sleep in the hope that my worst nightmares won't return.

SIX

Anika

____

"What? You don't remember me? Cuz I remember you. You're Big J's girl, right?"

Anika is staring at the man, heart racing, fear freezing her limbs.

And apparently her vocal cords. Of course she remembers him.

His name is Frankie, a short young man with a Boston accent and tattoos everywhere, including a four-leaf clover under his right eye. One of Jay's dealer buddies. She's only met him once, one night when she showed up to Jay's place to surprise him. Anika could never forget the way Frankie looked at her, like a piece of meat he wanted to shred with his teeth.

Same as he's looking at her now, with an unsettling smile that goes mostly sideways.

"Frankie," she says, finally answering his question. "Jay's friend."

"Yeah, how you been? Ain't seen ya since Jay dipped. Say, you ain't seen him, have ya?"

Another chill goes through her. Frankie's dark eyes are

33

burning through her, probing for a sign that she knows something about what happened to Jay.

She can't remember anything after he kicked in the door. She woke up at her place the following morning. She waited two days to hear from him, but nothing.

Anika drove by his apartment one night and saw police inside, some leaving with boxes. She got a call the next day from a detective asking to meet her. The cops were looking for Jay, wondering if she'd seen him. Sources said he vanished with a sizable sum of drugs and money.

She can't remember her answers, only that one of the detectives, the female, handed her a card and asked Anika to call if she remembered anything.

"No," she says. "I haven't. Have you?"

"No. Weird as hell, don't ya think?"

"Yeah."

She fidgets with the bracelet on her left wrist.

He notices.

She stops.

His eyes meet hers. "Man, everyone has been looking for you, the mysterious girlfriend."

"*Me?* Why?"

"I hear he owed some people big."

Anika wonders if Jay owed him, though she doesn't think so. He'd seemed friendly with Frankie that time she saw them together.

A flash of a memory, him saying, "These are scary people. I can't —"

It's gone just as quick as it came. She wonders if it's from the missing moments before he vanished. Does she know where he went? And if so, why has she forgotten?

"I don't know anything about that," Anika says, wondering if that's why he's here.

"Relax." Frankie smiles. "I ain't gonna tell nobody I seen ya."

She wonders why he's at her restaurant. Coincidence, or was he looking for her? And if so, why? "What can I get you?"

He orders a draft beer. She asks if he wants time to look over the menu, but he's ready to order a burger and fries.

She puts his order into the kitchen, then goes to the bar to ask Jenny for a draft. Jenny has two customers and looks bored out of her mind.

"How's it going?" Jenny asks.

She's always been cordial, but Jenny's friends with both Jolene and Candi, so Anika resists the urge to bitch about the table situation.

"Just a slow day," she says.

"Tell me about it." Jenny finishes filling the glass and returns the nozzle to its spot.

Anika grabs the glass and realizes she's shaking.

Calm down. He doesn't know anything.

Know? *What is there to know?*

Relax. Just bring him his beer and see what else he has to say.

Anika's always trusted her inner voice. It's been there with her for as long as she can remember, ever since her traumatic childhood. She's not sure if it's some higher power guiding her; some calm, rational part of her brain; or hell, maybe she's schizo and it's another personality, but she's learned to listen when it issues an order.

"You okay?" Jenny asks.

"Yeah, just a migraine."

She returns to the table and hands Frankie his frosty mug.

He thanks her, takes a sip, then pops a pill into his mouth and swallows.

He catches her looking at him. "Well, if your guy just up and went, I'm guessing you need a hookup?"

"Huh?" Anika asks.

He reaches into his jacket pocket and pulls out a bottle. "The pills."

She looks around to make sure nobody's paying attention. "I ... I don't need any."

"Ah." He winks and returns the pills to his pocket. "Gotcha."

"For real. I ... don't need them anymore."

"You sure?" He eyes her shaking hands. "You look a little off."

"I'm sure."

"Okay." But the way he's looking at her, she knows he doesn't believe her.

Anika heads back to the kitchen to get away from his overly familiar gaze. She paces, waiting on Sam to finish cooking Frankie's order.

Calm the hell down. You're freaking out over nothing.

What if he knows?

That word again — knows.

What the hell did I do?

The voice is silent.

"Order up," Sam shouts out of habit, even though Anika is right there. He sets the meal on the line and gives her a nod.

"Thanks."

Back at her station, Anika places the burger and fries in front of Frankie, then asks if she can get him anything else.

Jenny is seating an older couple in her station.

Frankie looks around the table, finds the ketchup next to the salt and pepper, and shakes his head. "I'm good."

She starts to turn, but then he says, "Wait."

"Yes?"

He takes four long swallows to finish his beer, then says, "I'll take another."

"Sure thing." Anika goes to the old couple and gets their drink orders.

Then she brings Frankie his second beer, hoping he'll let her be. He stops her instead. "So, you really ain't seen him 'round?"

"No."

"Could be some big money in it if you have."

"I haven't seen him. Same as I told the cops. They're saying he took some stuff, but I don't know anything. Jay never involved me in that stuff."

"Well, except when *you* needed that stuff."

"I didn't take … what he sold. And if I knew anything about where he took off to, I wouldn't be here — I'd be off in the Bahamas or wherever he disappeared to." Anika is pissed and done playing sweet. "Will there be anything else?"

Frankie looks at her, stunned.

"Okay, then," she says, pulling his check from her pocket. "Thank you."

She leaves before he can say anything else, breathes a sigh of relief, and readies a smile for the old couple as she checks on them.

The man is asking her about some dessert the restaurant used to have when she spies Frankie from the corner of her eye, getting up and approaching her.

She pretends not to notice, keeping her attention glued to the old man. She listens as he describes some blueberry pastry he'd once had there, he thinks, but it's hard to focus on him with Frankie coming closer.

Inches away, she braces for attack, like he might shiv her.

But she can't show fear. Has to keep pretending she can't even see him.

He passes by without incident and Anika breathes a sigh of relief before telling the old man that she'll check with the cook to see if they have anything like that, even though she knows for sure that Sam will say, *Hell no.*

After delivering the disappointing news, and taking the old man's order for an ice cream sundae, Anika goes to clean Frankie's table.

She gathers his thirty bucks along with the check, but then she sees something underneath it. A small plastic bag with a half-dozen pills. And under that, a scrap of paper with Frankie's number.

Damn it.

She scoops the pills, and his number, into her pocket before anyone sees her.

I'm not going to use them.

I'm not going to use them.

Oh yeah? Then why are they in your pocket?

CHELSEA'S HOUSE is a forty-minute drive, her place tucked away in a beautiful gated community called Tuxedo Hills.

It's dusk when Anika arrives. She feels like an intruder as she pulls her car up behind a black BMW SUV, wondering if it belongs to Chelsea or her husband, Stuart Preston, a renowned plastic surgeon.

She doesn't like Stuart, but mostly because he judges her, especially after she asked him for a small loan in a moment of weakness. He gave her the money and said she could keep it, but Anika could see the pity and judgment in his eyes. She shouldn't have ever taken a cent. He'll always look at her the same, no matter how much she changes or gets her shit together.

A teenage girl opens the door, a light-skinned black girl with her hair in a ponytail. A wide smile with blue braces matches her school uniform shirt.

"You must be Anika!"

"Hi," Anika says, looking for her sister but not seeing her.

"She's changing Emery."

"Ah."

The girl holds out her hand. "I'm Rae. I watch Emery when Chelsea has meetings."

"Ah, nice to meet you, Rae," Anika says, shaking her hand.

"Okay, I've gotta get home. My boyfriend's gonna call." Her voice is raspy, but her personality bubbly. She reminds Anika of Chelsea at her age.

"Ah, don't wanna keep him waiting," Anika says.

Rae shouts, "Okay, I'll see you Sunday, Chelsea!"

"Bye, honey. Thanks again."

"Anytime!" She grabs a big purple bag off Chelsea's dark leather couch and bounds toward the door. "Nice meeting you."

Anika sits and waits in the living room, admiring the design choices. The house is spacious, a far cry from where she grew up with Chelsea — a rundown four-bedroom ranch house in a rundown part of town.

Their foster parents had little, but they did their best, and were a hell of a lot better than either of the families the girls were born into. Not that Anika's mom was bad. She was a saint, from what Anika can remember. But Chelsea's parents were in jail for selling drugs and child endangerment. She went into the system and ended up with Ed and Judy Reynolds one year before Anika wound up in the same place.

"To what do I owe the pleasure?" Chelsea asks as she enters the living room holding her beautiful daughter against her chest.

The toddler looks at Anika with big brown eyes. Her curly brown hair is long and thick, tied with pink bows that match her princess dress with a unicorn on the front.

"Oh my God, she's getting so big." Anika stands to hug Chelsea and get a closer look at Emery.

"Sixteen months today." Chelsea shows Anika her perfect smile, golden eyes warm, reminding her how much she's missed her sister.

"Do you want to hold her?" Chelsea asks.

Anika thinks of the pills in the baggie sitting in her glove compartment and feels an icy sting of shame. "Okay," she says, taking the girl into her hands.

Emery looks confused, then bursts into tears.

Anika immediately hands her back. "Okay, maybe not."

Chelsea laughs. "I'm sorry, someone missed her nap today. And by someone, I mean me. But also her. We're both too tired."

Anika laughs. "I'm sorry, I just stopped by to say hi."

"Oh, no worries. I'm good. This little one, though, will be going down soon."

Emery points at a stuffed dog on the ground.

Chelsea puts her down and she crawls to the animal. Emery starts chewing on one of the dog's paws while laughing.

"Want anything to drink?" Chelsea leads her to the kitchen and opens the stainless steel fridge with a computer screen on the front.

The fridge is perfectly lit. Bright, with neatly lined rows

of bottles, fancy flavored water that's well outside Anika's budget, an assortment of vaguely healthy-looking drinks, and food stacked in perfectly organized plastic cubes.

Anika thinks of her own fridge at home with an expired half-gallon of milk, a near empty pitcher of lemonade, ancient lunch meat, wilted lettuce, and a box of half-eaten pizza that's probably rock hard. Not looking even a fraction as nice as Chelsea's fridge, or a tenth as well-stocked.

Anika says she'll take one of the fancy flavored bottles of water.

It's blueberry and bitter, but Anika pretends to like it.

"How are you?" Chelsea says, looking Anika up and down. "You look good."

It makes her self-conscious, knowing she's nowhere near as pretty as her foster sister. Anika is almost sickly pale, mousy with flat blonde hair pulled back in a tight ponytail, dark green eyes that seem almost lifeless whenever she looks in a mirror. Her black jeans and polo both feel greasy and reek like the restaurant.

Chelsea has healthy-looking mocha skin and curly dark hair, hanging loosely over her shoulders. Effortlessly beautiful, like always. Even as a tomboy teenager. She's in cozy jeans and a blush-colored sweater. Everything looks amazing on her.

"Thanks. You look great! How are you, and Stuart?"

"Busy, but good. He's working late."

Anika isn't sure what a plastic surgeon might be doing at this hour, but isn't about to ask and feel stupid. Maybe he works at the hospital sometimes.

"So," Chelsea says, "what brings you all the way out here? You okay?"

"It's been a while since I've seen you. I got off early, so I figured I'd visit."

Chelsea is looking at Anika with an expression of pity she can't stand. Her sister is only a year older, but has always acted like the responsible elder sibling, while Anika has always felt like a screw-up, wayward child.

Chelsea did well in school while Anika struggled to pay attention.

Chelsea spent her time studying and working part-time jobs while Anika hung out with a string of loser boyfriends, often getting high.

Chelsea went to college and got a degree in business, then went on to launch a successful business selling beauty products. She married a rich doctor and has a lovely little girl while Anika works a job she hates, lives in a tiny apartment, and has no one to love her.

"So, what's new?" Chelsea leads her back into the living room, sits on the couch, and turns on the TV for Emery — some cartoon Anika doesn't recognize.

"Not much. Work was crazy today."

"Still at that restaurant?"

"Yeah." *Can't get a better job because I failed at school, and life.*

"You still going out with that guy? What was his name? James?"

"Jay," Anika corrects. Chelsea didn't like him, even though she only knew what Anika told her. She never should have mentioned his anger issues or drug use. "And no, I dumped him."

Another pathetic lie.

Can't even keep a druggie loser boyfriend? What is wrong with you, girl?

"Good. And ... how are you?"

"You mean am I still taking pills?"

Chelsea gives Anika her uncomfortable face, crosses

one hand over the other while pursing her lips. "Yes. Last time I saw you, you had me worried."

"Been clean ninety-two days."

"Wow. Really?" Now she's beaming. "Is that why I haven't heard from you? You going to meetings now?"

"I'm doing it on my own."

"You sure that's a good idea?" Again, her smile is forced.

"I tried the meeting thing and between the scary people looking at me weird and the scarier people selling drugs in the parking lot. no thanks."

"Maybe you need a better neighborhood. Come to a meeting out here. I'll go with you."

"Thanks, sis. I appreciate it, but I'm doing well. I promise."

"Good."

Her phone rings. Chelsea grabs it off the kitchen counter and looks at the screen. "Can you watch Emery for a second? I have to take this."

"Sure."

Chelsea disappears down the hall toward her office, her voice fading while Anika stares at the TV screen, then at Emery engrossed in her cartoon.

She laughs at a cat getting his head stuck in a small box. Her giggle is sweet and innocent, reminding Anika of her own stolen youth.

She envies her sister having a chance to live a better childhood vicariously through her daughter. Envies her nice house, stable job and marriage. Then hates herself for the jealousy.

Anika wants her sister to be happy.

But a voice in her head says, *This should've been yours.*

No, Chelsea deserves all the happiness she has. She went through hell, too.

Not like you. She didn't watch her father kill her mother before finishing himself.

Stop it. I don't envy Chelsea. She's a good person, and I'm happy for her.

Yeah, but you're *not happy. You're miserable, admit it. The sooner you're honest about it, the sooner you can help yourself.*

How?

You know.

The pills?

One pill won't kill you. It'll make you happy.

Stop it.

"Anika?" Chelsea asks.

She's confused. Outside, standing on the porch, with no memory as to how she got out here. Anika lies to cover her confusion. She can't admit to having no memory of walking outside. "Sorry, I needed some fresh air. I was starting to have a panic attack."

Anika can see Chelsea's disbelief in her eyes.

She looks down at the plastic bag in Anika's hand and says, "What's that?"

She freezes.

What the hell? Did I take a pill and not even remember it?

"Nothing," Anika says. "I need to go."

"Wait!"

But Anika is walking to her car before she starts crying, or before her sister figures out that she's holding pills.

"I don't feel well. I really need to leave. I'm sorry."

She's crying, despite trying like hell not to.

"You don't need to go. You can tell me."

Anika shakes her head. "It's okay. I swear."

She gets in her car and pulls out of her sister's driveway, tears streaming down her face as she wonders what the hell is always so wrong with her.

SEVEN

Delaney

It's Dad's birthday, or I wouldn't even be here.

It's hard enough that I have to visit him once a month. It takes days to recover because he's insufferable when himself, always avoiding my questions about where my mom might have gone off to. But this extra visit is too much, and I struggle to get out of the car.

I sit in the parking lot, staring at the Morning Sun, a pretty name for a sad place to die.

I consider leaving. There's an excellent chance he won't even miss me. Sometimes I come and he remembers. Most times lately, not.

And, depending on the visit, I'm not sure which is worse.

I summon the courage, telling myself I'll treat myself tonight and get extra drunk. Maybe hit that new restaurant downtown with the coffee rub on their filet. Eat well and drink even better. Then go home and sleep for a day or two.

I say *hi* to Nancy working the front desk. A nice,

heavyset black woman in her late forties. She smiles at me, palming her phone call. "Hey, Del. How's it going?"

"Good. You?"

"Good, sweetheart. Keshawn says to tell you thank you. You really saved his ass."

"No problem. Glad I could help."

"My nephew's a good boy. He insists on paying you back, once he's back on his feet. Shouldn't be too long now that he can work."

"No need to pay me back. That car was taking up space," I lie. A classic '68 Mustang. The car needed work, but I could've easily sold it for some decent scratch. But her nephew was struggling to get out of a bad situation in the south side projects, and it felt like the right thing to do since I wasn't using it. Nancy's always been nice to me.

"Well, it was everything to him. You're too sweet."

"Please continue to hold," she says in her most professional voice.

"How's Dad? Is he cogent?"

Nancy shakes her head. "Not a good day, honey."

"He in his room?"

"No, they're having a party for him in the restaurant."

"Okay, thanks." I spot a paperback on the desk. There's a bare-chested werebear on the front cover holding a buxom woman in obvious ecstasy.

"Still reading the smut?" I tease.

"It's spicy romance," she corrects me with a grin. "*Literary* spicy romance."

"Mmm-hmm," I say, heading toward my father's party.

If there's one thing I can say about this place, other than its excellent staff, their cafeteria looks and feels like a restaurant. When Father is having his good days, he invites me to eat lunch or dinner with him. The food is excellent, considering what it is and where it came from.

I smile at old folks as I pass them.

I've always felt a kinship with the elderly, even as a child. I felt like I was born a generation or two late. Maybe it's because my parents were old when they had me, and most of the people in Father's church were on the far side of life, so it was all I knew for a long time. I've always had an overwhelming and bittersweet nostalgia for good old days I wasn't a part of.

Weird, because I doubt I'd have fared all that well in the forties, fifties, or sixties. A loudmouth like me might've had trouble staying "in my place."

But it's not like I feel at home in the present, even if my gruff manners are more acceptable.

I usually loathe small talk, but the folks here seem to appreciate visitors, and as much as I hate most people, I like to see the elderly smiling.

I make it to the restaurant and see a pair of tables pushed together with a small crowd of Father's friends gathered around it.

Someone put a birthday hat on him, and he doesn't look pleased. His cake reads *Happy 70th* even though he looks a decade and a half older than that.

It never fails to surprise each time I see him with yet another month behind us. He's still the father of my youth in my mind. A large, looming figure, imposing in stature. A deep voice, a lantern jaw, and intense azure eyes. He never seemed all that old back then, despite his age. Youthful if anything, with energy to spare.

Now he's a shell of that man.

Still broad shouldered, now they slump forward. His face is gaunt, and his hair gray wisps. His fingers are knotted in arthritic pain. I'd swear he's smaller than I remember, as if someone shrank his body.

There are four female and two male residents sitting

with him, plus Rosita, a thirty-something Puerto Rican nurse with a short crewcut and soft brown eyes, standing beside him. Some days she's the only one Father will let look after him.

"Look who's come to visit you on your birthday."

"Oh, it's Del," says one of the residents, giving me a gummy grin, followed by a great big hug like I'm her daughter or grandchild.

"Hello, Edna," I say, avoiding a mouthful of poofy gray hair as I return the hug.

Father looks up at me, and though he manages the faintest of smiles, I see no recognition in his eyes.

"Hi," I say with a small wave.

He nods, but there aren't any words and I'm not surprised. He speaks less each time I come. Seems a bit weaker, especially now that he's in a wheelchair after falling in the shower and being told he needs to stay off his feet.

I wonder how long it will be until he dies.

I feel awful thinking of my father as a burden, but then I remind myself of all the shitty things he's done. To me and everyone else. Sometimes that helps with the guilt.

"Would you like some cake?" Rosita asks.

Everyone's already had theirs. I don't want to prolong the party, especially with Father barely here. He either rambles incoherently or sits in stony silence when he doesn't remember me.

"No thanks. I just came to wish him a happy birthday."

Rosita turns to him. "Do you want Del to walk in the garden with you?"

Father looks at me, then Rosita. There's an uncomfortable look in his eyes. Maybe fear?

He shakes his head. "I'm tired."

"But she drove all this way to see you."

"I'm tired!" He raises his voice, not nearly as booming as it used to be, but still drawing the attention of everyone around us.

The other residents are eyeing me with pity. Most of them have yet to lose their minds so they can see the difficulty of this scene.

Rosita mouths *sorry* and wheels my father away from the table.

I didn't want to spend all day here, but I'm still annoyed that he barely wanted a minute with me. I head back the way I came, approaching Nancy to say goodbye. She gives me a look and I know that bad news is about to spill out of her mouth.

"Pam wants to talk."

I cast a glance towards the offices and see her peering through an open door.

"Fuck," I say out loud without really meaning to.

"Sorry. Want me to tell her you're busy?"

"Nah, I've been blowing off her calls. Can't ignore billing forever."

"Don't you worry. She ain't gonna get rid of your old man over you being a little late."

I nod, not wanting to admit that I'm actually three months behind. And Pam has been plenty patient already.

I wave bye, then head to Pam's office.

Pam is a thin, pale woman in her late forties. She's sitting behind her desk, lips tight pursed, hair pulled into an even tighter bun. Her dresses are shapeless enough to sleep in.

She peers at me through her thick glasses. "Did you change your number?"

Pam can never be direct, always asking some passive-aggressive question instead of something like, *So, why are you blowing me off?*

"No, sorry. Been busy."

"Business picking up?"

I know what she's thinking. "Business, yeah. Paying customers, not so much."

"Listen, Del, I'm not going to sugarcoat this. I need to see some effort from you to pay or my boss will eject your dad from this establishment. Have you ever considered a more affordable facility?"

"You think I want to spend all my money on this place? I don't, and if I'm being honest, my father sure as hell doesn't deserve the care you all provide, but … I've seen some of the horror stories in the news. And at least you take care of him. Please, bear with me until I can sort things out. How much to satisfy your boss?"

"At least one month."

I reach into my purse and pull out the only card with any credit left. "Run one month now and I'll get more to you next week. I have a couple checks waiting to clear."

This is a total lie, but what else am I gonna do?

She takes my card without a word, then turns to a second desk with a computer on the top.

She punches my number in, then punches it in again.

Declined.

Shit.

Pam turns to me, issuing the same tiny sigh that always sits like a splinter in my skin. "Do you have another one?"

"Not on me, but I can call you when I get home."

She stares as if trying to decide how full of shit I might be. We both know the truth, but Pam's too polite to say so out loud.

"I need to hear from you by tomorrow at noon, okay?"

She's holding my card, as if waiting for me to agree before handing it back.

"Yes, ma'am," I say, faking a smile.

She hands me my card and I leave, needing to check my balance before getting thoroughly drunk.

Not necessarily in that order.

EIGHT

Delaney

I had planned to eat and drink myself stupid, but instead I did the responsible thing and checked my bank account online first.

Turns out a check from a client bounced and that triggered a round of stupid charges on my account, each one sending me deeper into the red.

Through logistics I can't possibly understand other than some colossal idiocy or evil intent of the bank's AI system, they did chargebacks on my smaller purchases instead of the one big one they should've hit me for.

I can't resolve the issue online, because of course not, so I've been on the phone with the bank waiting for a human. Forty-three minutes of painful Muzak intermittently interrupted every minute by a voice who offers me hope, only to take it away with yet another reminder.

Thank you for waiting. Your call will be taken in the order it was received.

"I *know* I'm on hold, you fuckers."

I want to murder whoever dreamed up automated phone trees, then travel back in time and eliminate their ancestors, scorching the earth of their seed so they may never be born and I can forever rid the world of their kind.

Finally, a human voice, though it's an accent I can barely understand. *Jimmy.*

I tell Jimmy the situation.

Of course, *he* can't help me.

He has to put me through to someone in another department, which will mean another "short wait."

And the phone clicks.

My heart's in my throat as I wait for some sign that my call was still live.

But of course it's been dropped.

So I pitch my phone across the room with a scream.

Pumpkin, sitting on the sill in a warm spot, looks up from grooming himself to give me a confused look.

"Technology sucks, Pumpkin."

Pumpkin, apparently not in the mood to hear me whine, returns to his grooming.

I grab my phone off the floor, praying it isn't broken.

I got a good case, so it's still in working condition. But the battery was low, so I charge it before trying the bank again.

Once it has enough juice, I call the bank back only to be informed that I should try again tomorrow during business hours.

Because of fucking course.

Annoyed because now I have to wait another day, or maybe even until Monday since banks are closed on the weekend, and who knows how many additional charges will appear between now and then, I decide to call the client who put me in this position.

Claire Hanson hired me to see if her fiancé, Christian Powell, was a decent guy.

She runs a successful online business, helping people

with small e-commerce sites optimize their traffic. She's in her late fifties, while her beau is a bit too good-looking, too charming, and a little young to seem like the real deal.

In other words, Claire was worried he was out for her money.

Spoiler alert, he was.

Not only that, the guy was stringing along several other women.

Real asshole.

I spent a few days digging up enough to give Claire a definitive answer, no psychic powers required. It would've been a simple case, but she was so pissed, I had to spend another three weeks wedging that shovel in deeper. She wanted everything she could get on this guy, so she could burn his scam to the ground.

I spent a month on her case, working long hours, talking to everyone in this dickhead's life, until I had enough evidence for Claire.

How she planned to take him down was no concern of mine. Probably a public embarrassment, maybe an exposé in the news, whatever. I gave her all the ammo she needed. It's not like she was going to have him killed.

Claire was happy and paid on time.

But her check bounced and I need to know why.

She answers her phone on the second ring and I tell her the situation, assuming it's a fixable mistake. But, judging from her anguish-ridden voice, that's not about to happen.

"I'm sorry. He emptied my accounts."

"How?"

"I don't know, but he got access to everything and now he's disappeared."

She goes into detail, so much that I'm sick to my

stomach by the time she's done. I want to hurt this guy, slowly.

"Fuck. I'm so sorry, Claire."

"Me too. I'm working with the police to try and recover what I can, but … I'm not sure how long it'll take. Or how long until I can pay you back."

Claire cries, telling me how stupid she feels. She should've known better, the signs were there.

"You're not stupid at all. You hired me before getting married."

She thinks he must've found out. Had cloned her phone and was basically privy to everything she was doing, including hiring me.

She apologizes and promises to make good on her debt.

I feel awful. Such a betrayal cuts deep; it'll impact her financially in the present, and emotionally for the rest of her life. Claire might never recover from this, and it kills me.

I want to help, but what can I do?

The words spill out of my mouth before I even think them through.

"Don't worry about paying me back. We're good."

"I can't do that."

No, idiot, she's right. You can't afford to do that! This guy fucked you both!

"It's okay," I lie. "Just focus on getting your stuff back so we can nail this asshole. You need anything else, don't hesitate to call."

Wait, you're going to do more free work for her? What the hell are you thinking?

"Thank you, Del. God bless you."

I hang up.

I'm not counting on any blessings. If recent events —

and by recent I mean my entire life — are anything to go by, God hates my shit.

I plug my phone back into the charger and head down to the pool with a six-pack.

~

I WAKE to the sound of my phone ringing.

Why the hell didn't I turn it off?

Oh, yeah, because I passed out before I could get undressed.

I pick it up and look at the name and number, surprised.

"Hello?" I say, trying not to sound as shitty as I feel.

"Hi, Del. It's Marsha Sutherland. I wanted to apologize for yesterday. My husband had no right to attack you like that."

"It's okay, really."

"He's a bit more cynical than I am. He's used to people trying to screw him over, so he's always expecting it. He didn't even want me to call you. I thought he was fine with it. Had no idea he only agreed so he could have a chance to pull his little stunt. I really am sorry."

"There are a lot of shady psychics out there. Most, in fact. No hard feelings, Mrs. Sutherland. And best of luck finding your son. I mean that."

"I still want to hire you."

"What?"

"You helped find that girl when everybody else had given up. Frankly, I think everybody else is done looking for Jay. Including his father. Part of me understands. He has his problems. But he's my son, and *I can't* give up on him. No matter what he's done, he'll always be my little boy. I believe in redemption. Do you, Ms. West?"

I think about my father's fall from grace and want to say no, some people can never be redeemed. But I lie and tell her what she wants to hear.

"Yes."

"And a mother deserves to know whether her son is alive and well, right?"

"Yes, of course."

"Please, Ms. West. I'll pay twice your fee. Just … help me."

I have no desire to deal with her husband's negativity again, but the gig would cover my father's bills. And I'd be helping a mother find her son, or at least get some closure.

"I'll take your case."

"God bless you." It sounds like that's all she can say without crying.

A small part of me, the kid who once believed so fervently, wonders if God is working through His mysterious ways.

I lost one client, only to have this one offer twice my rate.

Maybe my luck is finally changing.

Or maybe I stopped thinking like that since it's always an invitation for shit to go tits up again.

NINE

Anika (Age 5)

Anika wakes up to crying.

She's supposed to ignore it, pretend it's not happening.

But it's her mother, and she *can't*.

What if he's hurting her — again?

Anika crawls out of bed, clutching her teddy bear, Edwin, and sneaks to the end of the stairs and sits, curling up into as small a ball as possible in the shadows just in case Daddy looks up.

They're in the kitchen.

She can only see his back. He shouts, "Why the hell not?"

Anika's not sure what he's asking about. It's Saturday night, and Daddy always comes home late on Saturday night. Late and angry.

Not that he isn't mad on other nights. But he's not usually this loud. Something about Saturday changed him.

Her father moves out of view.

Anika hears pots and pans smashing against the counter.

"I guess I have to do *everything* myself," he yells, slamming cupboards, "just like always!"

"I'm sorry. I didn't know you'd be hungry. You usually eat with the boys on Saturday." Mommy sounds like she's about to cry.

"Well, I didn't get to eat tonight. And that's not the point."

"If I knew, I would've—"

"I slave away all day while you sit on your ass. Is it too much to ask for a few fucking meals just in case? This isn't the first time, Marie. Not by a long shot. You should be prepared."

"I'm sorry, I haven't been feeling well. I've been tired."

More slamming pots and pans.

Anika flinches.

Mommy comes into view.

She looks up, right at her daughter.

Anika freezes. She's not sure if Mommy can see her or not.

Mommy turns away, talking again. "What do you want? I'll make it."

"No, I'll do it myself. Go to bed. God knows I'd hate for you to be *tired.*"

He laughs, a scary little giggle that Anika's never heard before.

Just leave, Mommy. Go to bed like he said.

Mommy starts to leave the kitchen.

Daddy says, "That's right, lazy bitch."

Mommy stops.

No, Mommy. Don't stop. Come to bed.

Mommy turns around.

No, Mommy.

Mommy does the one thing she should never ever do when Daddy's like this.

She talks back.

"I'm not lazy."

"What?"

No, Mommy, don't say anything. Walk away.

Anika watches her mother disappear from view.

No, no, no.

A loud SMACK!

Mommy stumbles back, falling into Anika's view.

Daddy enters the picture, looking madder than she's ever seen him.

Anika wants Mommy to get up and run, but she isn't getting up. Mommy looks like she might be hurt, her hand pressed to her head.

He looks down at her. "You fucking cunt."

He gets on his knees and wraps his hands around her throat.

He's choking her!

Anika knows she shouldn't do or say anything, not after last time. But she can't just sit there hiding while Daddy hurts Mommy.

"Get off her!"

Daddy stops choking Mommy and looks up.

His eyes are scary and wide.

He stands.

And runs up the stairs.

Anika screams as she runs to her room.

"No, Daddy! No!"

She doesn't lock the door because there isn't enough time. And Daddy would only be madder if she did.

She slides under the bed, crying as she hears her door burst open and slam against the wall.

"Anika!"

"I'm sorry, Daddy."

"Come out from under that bed or I swear to Christ I will drag you out."

"Please, Daddy, I'm sorry."

"Come out. *Now*."

She holds Edwin tight, crying, "Please, Daddy, I'm sorry. I just didn't want—"

He grabs her by the hair and yanks hard.

Anika screams.

Daddy throws her on the bed and stares down at her. "What are you doing up?"

His breath is hot and stinky, like it always is when he's like this.

"I'm sorry. I heard Mommy crying and I was scared."

He stops, staring at her, as if confused, maybe trying to decide if he should hit her or not.

He doesn't do that often. But when he does …

"Simon!" Mommy's footsteps are coming up the stairs fast.

He turns around, slams the door and locks it.

"Simon!" Mommy calls from the other side, banging on the door. "Leave her alone or I'm calling the cops."

He laughs. "*Relax*, I'm not gonna hurt her! But, yeah, feel free to make that call, honey. Tell 'em I said *hi* while you're at it."

He gives her another mean little laugh. Of course Daddy doesn't care if she calls the cops. He *is* a cop.

"Open the door, Simon. Please. I'm sorry."

He looks down at Anika and points a finger. "Don't ever interfere again when Mommy and I are talking. You stay in bed. Understand me?"

"Yes, Daddy."

"You said that last time, and it seems you forgot. How can we make sure you remember?"

"I promise. I won't forget."

He looks at Anika for a long moment while she's shaking.

Anika peed her pants, though she's not sure if he's noticed.

She's holding her teddy bear tight, like Edwin can protect her. Maybe not, but at least he understands.

Daddy grabs Edwin.

She cries out and reaches for the teddy.

Daddy shoves her back on the bed and holds Edwin high enough that she can't reach him even if she stands on her tippy toes.

"Ah, maybe you need something to remind you not to interfere again. What do you say?"

Anika's not sure what he means, but she thinks he's about to take Edwin.

"Please, Daddy, I'll remember."

He holds her bear toward her, smiling. She thinks it's friendly, like he sometimes is when he's not like this.

She reaches out to take Edwin.

He grabs the teddy's head and rips it off his body.

"Edwin!"

Daddy holds the bear's head, shaking it in front of her. "You did this."

Anika turns her head, crying.

"Look at it! I want you to remember. This is what happens when you disobey me. Do you hear me?"

She can't look.

"Look!"

Anika does, her gut twisting as she sees the stuffing hanging out of Edwin's neck.

There's no way he can ever be fixed. And it's all her fault.

"Say it with me, honey. This is what happens when I disobey."

Anika can't talk, too many tears.

"Say it," Daddy commands her, shoving Edwin's head hard against Anika's cheek. "Say it."

"This is what happens when I disobey."

He throws Edwin's head, then body, at her.

"Now I think you will remember."

She cries as she holds her bear's head and body against her chest as if squeezing him tight might fix him.

She wants to scream out that she hates Daddy.

She wants to tell him to leave her and Mommy alone.

But Anika can only cry as he leaves, shutting the door.

"What did you—"

"I didn't do anything," Daddy says, cutting Mommy off. "Now let's finish our conversation."

They go downstairs.

Anika is holding Edwin tight still. "I'm sooooooo sorry."

She knows teddy bears aren't real, but Edwin is different. He's always been there for her. He talks to her late at night when she's scared and alone.

At least he used to.

"Please, Edwin, don't die."

A voice whispers from the shadows in the corner of her room, surprising her.

She looks over, confused because it's so familiar. Edwin's voice, low and deep, like a friendly old man.

Except now he sounds angry.

"I'm not dead, dear."

She stares at the darkness.

"Edwin?"

Something steps out of the shadows.

TEN

Anika (Now)

Anika wakes from her dream, the childhood memory already fading into a fog of confusion.

Something about her parents.

She misses her mother still.

She looks at the bag of pills on her nightstand. She was good, didn't open it or take any. At least not that she remembers.

But she also didn't flush them.

Yet.

Instead, Anika took a Xanax to calm herself after getting home from Chelsea's. Two before passing out.

She showers and gets ready for work, still lethargic, limbs heavy and mind dull. She prays that the restaurant isn't slammed. She doesn't usually hope for a slow day, but Anika's not sure she can function much in her current state.

She drives to work, slowly and carefully, and goes inside to find Ken freaking out on the phone as he runs his hands through his few tufts of hair.

"Well, tell her to call as soon as she can."

He looks at Anika as he hangs up. "Thank God *you* showed up."

"What?"

"Candi, Thom, and Erica all called in."

"I'm the only one on?"

He nods. "For now. Oh, and there's a kid's birthday in an hour. A party of thirty."

Anika wants to cry.

A FEW HOURS in and she's barely hanging on. It's been a shit show of a day where everything that could go wrong has. She's dropped food, screwed up not one but three orders, got yelled at once, and was on the verge of tears several times.

Fortunately, Ken gets a couple of servers to come in, and nobody from second shift bailed on their shift, so Anika is finally able to take a break at five.

She goes out to her car with a burger and a Coke, cranks some music, and closes her eyes as she finally finds some peace.

She's startled by a knock on her window. Drops her burger and loses it to scattered piles on the carpet. Glances up to see a scary bald white dude with an orange beard and dark brown eyes peering at her like a threat.

He's yelling something, then lifts his white tank top to reveal a pistol.

She reads his lips: *Roll down the window, bitch!*

Is this a carjacking, or ... does it have to do with Jay? The latter, of course. Frankie told someone, and now they're here to find out what she knows about Jay.

Or ... collect what he owes them.

Anika kills the music and rolls down her window, heart

racing.

He leans in, licking his gold-plated teeth. His face tattoo is a swastika.

"Where's he at?"

"Where's who?"

He slams his hands on the roof, so fast and so loud that Anika shrieks.

He leans in fast, before she can react, and has a hand around her throat as he comes in close. "Don't play fucking stupid, bitch. You know who."

"I haven't seen him in months."

"Well, if you do see your man, tell him Rufus is looking for his shit. And if I don't get my shit, I will kill him. And if I can't find him, I'll kill everyone he loves."

He tightens his grip on her throat. "You understand me?"

Anika nods.

He lets go.

Anika gasps and swallows. Then she looks at him, afraid to ask the obvious, but she has to.

"What does he have?"

He stares at her as though she's messing with him, before his expression changes and he gives her a sideways smile. "He knows what he's got. And I want it back, or I want fifteen grand. Three days. Since I can't find him, that means *you* have three days. Understand me?"

"I don't know where he is. And I don't have it, or the money."

"I have faith that you'll figure it out."

Anika tries to explain again, but he grabs her mouth and holds it tight, glaring at her.

"I want my drugs or the money. Not excuses. Run like him, or go to the cops, and my men will kill you. Your sister next. Then her kid and her doctor husband after that." Rufus pauses, as if capturing an epiphany. "Hey, he's a doctor, maybe you should ask *him* for money."

He raises a hand as if signaling to someone. A red light flashes in her eyes before settling on her chest. She freezes, staring down, unable to breathe or look at anything but the dot, certain it will be followed by a gunshot that will rip her chest open.

I can't die. Not like this.

But how do I give him what he wants when I don't have it?

Rufus pats her cheek, startling her attention back to him.

"Nod if you understand."

Anika nods.

He walks away.

The red dot disappears.

And she finally exhales.

~

SHE DOESN'T BOTHER GOING BACK into work. Once Rufus is gone, she tears out of the parking lot, driving aimlessly, eyes flicking to the rearview for any sign of someone following her.

Anika wonders if she would spot someone trained to follow her. Maybe they already know where she lives. Maybe they followed her home last night, when she wasn't looking for a tail.

She racks her brain, no idea what to do.

She doesn't know where the drugs are, nor does she have that kind of cash. She has fifteen hundred in the bank, give or take a few hundred in pending bills. And her maxed-out cards.

Run, says the voice in her head. *Just go. Start over somewhere else.*

But she doesn't have money to run, or to start over.

Then sell something.

What?

The necklace.

I can't sell Mom's necklace. It's the only thing I have left.

It's the only valuable thing you have. And what good is a necklace if you're not alive to remember its significance? Just sell the damned thing.

It's an antique necklace from her mom's side of the family, generations old. Anika's mother was planning on gifting it on her wedding day, but she never lived to see it.

Sell it and get him off your back.

She considers going to the police, but the threat holds her at bay and the cops hadn't exactly helped either of the times Anika had needed them most. They hadn't saved her mom from her dad, and they did nothing when she reported her foster parents' abuse.

She could call Chelsea, but she was scared of leading Rufus to her door.

What if he's already found her? What if he followed me there?

No, you can't involve her. She'll be pissed. She'll think you're on drugs again. She'll be disappointed and probably call you an idiot.

She wouldn't do that.

You saw that look in her eyes — she pitied you.

She thinks you're a fuck-up, same as always. This would only confirm it.

Anika can't think straight and needs something to relax, maybe a little something from her baggie, tucked away in the nightstand at home.

Anika feigns that she's sick. Ken is surprisingly cool with her request to go home and thanks her for the extra help. She has tomorrow off, so at least one day where she won't have to worry about Rufus — unless he already knows where she lives.

You should've moved away after Jay vanished. Just left the state and started over.

But you said not to, that it'd make me look guilty to the cops. You told me to stay.

Jay never knew where she lived. That voice in Anika's head had ordered her to keep it a secret. Easy enough when she practically lived at his place.

If Anika doesn't come up with the money, she'll have to leave town — assuming Rufus doesn't have people watching her.

And if they are, what the hell will I do?

Anika takes the scenic route until she's certain that no one has followed.

She gets home, locks her door, and grabs the gun she stole from Jay's place. He had so many he hadn't even noticed one missing.

She's never fired a gun, but she's watched enough video tutorials that she knows what to do. At least if someone comes for her, she has a chance of getting out alive.

She goes to her fridge, grabs a bottle of cold water, then gets her baggie from the nightstand. She draws a warm bath and lights a few scented candles. Her ritual after a hard day of work. Today she deserves it.

She sets the gun on the corner of the tub closest to her head, undresses, and grabs her bottle of water and a pill.

She sinks into the tub and lets the tension melt from her body.

She holds the pill in her hand, hesitating. Clean for ninety-three days. Anika hates tossing the accomplishment, but it's all she can do to keep from freaking the hell out.

It's okay. You're not doing it to get high. You're doing it to cope, to get through this shit.

She swallows the pill, waiting for her mind to meet her body in bliss.

ELEVEN

Delaney

I meet Marsha Sutherland at The Oasis Cafe on the southern beachside as gray clouds gather and a choppy surf rolls in.

The big booths are nice and private. She brings a key to Jay's apartment as I requested, so I can go through his things. The police have been there, as have his associates looking for their drugs, and the place is a mess that no one has cleaned. None of that matters. I just need to touch something of his. That might give me a vision of where he is.

I don't want to get her hopes up, so I let her know this only works about a quarter of the time. But there is a chance.

She apologizes again and fills me in on the basics of Jay as she understands them. She's surprisingly blunt when she tells me of his drug abuse and history of violence. She tried to get him help a few times, but he never followed through. Marsha kept trying, but her husband said she was wasting their time and money on a "lost cause."

She pays me double, and in cash to my surprise, then

asks for an estimate of how long I'll need before I have an answer. The longer it takes, the more she'll pay.

I thank her and tell her I'll get right to work. She asks that I call her directly — she doesn't want her husband to know she hired me.

I leave, deposit the cash in the bank, then call the nursing home to pay for two months, promising to get current soon while thanking Pam for her patience.

I'm sitting in my car afterwards, trying to decide if I should swing by Jay's place, or call my old friend, former detective Dusty Sweeney.

I make the call, greeted by Dusty's gravely, laid-back voice. "Hey, Del. Whadya need?"

"Why do you assume I *need* anything? Maybe I'm just calling to say hi."

He laughs before falling silent. I hear classic rock in the background of his bar, Sweeney's.

"Fine, I need to talk about a case I'm working. You busy?"

"It's dead until the lunch crowd, if you wanna stop by."

"I'm on my way."

~

SWEENEY'S IS an old-fashioned Irish pub in the heart of the bustling old downtown.

Lots of dark wood and shamrocks. A blue collar place and a cop bar at night, by virtue of being run by one of the city's most decorated former detectives. A cozy respite from the newer clubs that appeal to the younger crowds.

I walk inside, greeted by the smell of fried food. Dusty's already laid out a basket of his specialty onion rings and a frosted mug of beer for me at the bar. TVs line every wall, a variety of sports on the 24-hour channels, though they're all silent as Blues Traveler blares from the jukebox. Nobody else is in the bar, save for an old black man with an ancient hat and matching suit playing pool along the far wall.

"Thanks," I say, sitting on a stool and shoving one of the crunchy, spicy onion rings into my mouth.

"Damn, these are good," I say, washing it down with the beer. No fancy craft, only the classics and a few imports.

Everything about Dusty is big. From his stature — he's like six-foot-six — to his formidable gut, his bushy white beard and long white hair, and his deep, rattling voice that sounds like he wakes every morning and drinks six pints after chewing through a bag of rocks. He's in jeans, a long-sleeve white button-down, and a black leather vest which matches the patch over his left eye. His face is uncharacteristically red.

"Sunburn?" I ask.

"Yeah, made the mistake of going out in the sun."

"And you didn't burst into flames?" I tease.

"Just about. Miranda got a hair in her ass about suddenly wanting a garden in the front yard because the asshole across the street has one. So, yeah, that was my weekend. I really hate that fucker, Del. Always improving his house and making ours look inferior to Miranda."

"Sorry."

"I don't even know why she cares what the yard looks like. We're hardly ever home. I'm usually here and she's always at our daughter's, helping out with the baby."

"Some people actually take pride in their yard, Dusty."

"You can pave the whole damned thing over for all I care. The yard is for the neighbors, not me, and I don't even like mine. Half of them are narcing on one another to the homeowner's association. We never should've moved there. I got a letter yesterday because the fence around our AC is the wrong color. The wrong fucking color for a fence I didn't even want. Tell you what, I'm gonna cut my shrub into a middle finger. That'll show 'em."

I laugh as he rants for another few minutes. I can always count on Dusty to bitch, moan, and crack me up. Despite his cranky demeanor, the guy is somehow lovable. He was one hell of a cop. Lost his eye in the line of duty, responding to a school shooting while off duty like a damned hero.

"So, what brings you round these parts? Haven't seen you in a while."

"Been busy working, which brings me to the reason I'm here, other than your delightful company and greasy onion rings."

"Want more?" he asks as I shove the last one into my mouth.

"No, thanks," I say with my mouth full.

I tell him the situation, asking what he knows about Jay Sutherland. Despite being retired, Dusty still talks to his former associates all the time. If something's going down in the criminal underground, chances are Dusty knows as much, if not more, than the cops.

"Way I hear it, asshole disappeared with Rufus T's drugs."

"Rufus T?"

"Rufus Treadwell, neo-Nazi drug dealer who runs a crew of other scumbags on the south side. They've been trying to nail him for a while, but the man is slippery as a seal. Always finds someone small to take the hit for him."

"So, Jay was one of his dealers?"

"Not at first. Just some spoiled rich kid fucktard slumming with scumbags for street cred. Got hooked on coke, then in with one of Rufus's men. Owed some scratch. Rufus saw it as an opportunity to deal in some of the upper class places his men didn't have access to, so Jay started dealing on his behalf. Eventually, he up and left with fifteen grand's worth of drugs, and nobody's heard a peep."

"His parents think something happened to him."

"They hired you to find him?"

"Yeah."

"And, what's your gut say?"

"Just started, don't have an opinion, or hypothesis, yet. What do you think?"

"Well, guys in narcotics think one of two things — he took off with the drugs and is scared to come back, or he got robbed by some junkie and he's just gone."

"Usually when someone robs a dealer, they leave a body, don't they? Why go through the trouble of hiding it? Rival dealer trying to avoid a war?"

"I doubt it. Which is why I think he split. Asshole will show up, one way or another."

"Cops have any suspects if it's foul play?"

"They talked to a couple of his associates, and his girl-friend, but didn't like anyone for it. And, again, they don't have a body or any sign of a struggle at his place. So—"

"So he just left?"

"That's my guess."

"Any idea how I can find him? Anyone who might know where he went?"

"His girlfriend, but the cops watched her for a while. Even checked cell phone records and shit. Two months and not a peep. Which means he was super careful, which doesn't seem like the guy from what I hear, or he disap-peared without telling her where he went, or he's dead."

"What do you know about the girl?"

"Not much. Quiet, from what I heard. A waitress somewhere, don't remember the name. Could get it for you if ya need."

"Any other women in his life?"

"A few one-night stands, but nobody that seemed to know anything. Everyone thinks he was probably off doing the drugs. A few hoped he overdosed."

"Why's that?"

"He was an asshole, had some anger issues, smacked some of them girls around."

"How about the girlfriend? Did he smack *her* around?"

"Not that I know of. Not sure how close they were. Girl was quiet, not his type. Didn't seem to know what he was into. From what I hear, a quiet, sheltered girl. You talking to Rufus?"

"I might. Why?"

"He's brutal. Like Mexican cartel dangerous."

"I'll be fine."

He shakes his head. "I'm serious, Del. Be careful with this one. Maybe don't try so hard. If the world is one asshole short, is that really a problem?"

"Is that how you would've handled the case?"

"I didn't get a choice in my cases. You do. I also had the entire force behind me, so a guy like Rufus knows to watch out."

"I've got a particularly nasty cat named Pumpkin that Rufus will *not* want to fuck with."

I long for his laugh, but he looks too concerned.

"I'll be careful."

"You've got my number if you run into trouble."

"Thank you." I dig in my pocket and fish out a twenty.

"It's on the house, Del."

"I insist." I push the bill across the bar.

"Your money's no good here, kid. You're family."

Dusty's always had a soft spot for me, ever since he helped me out of a few jams when I was a rebellious teen trying my damnedest to let trouble find me. A beat officer at the time, and one of the few adults who gave enough of a damn to hear me. He could've easily arrested me for some of the shit I did. Instead he was like a mentor, setting me straight and giving me some much needed life advice.

"You getting soft in your old age, Dusty?"

"I'm trying to be nice, ya asshole."

I laugh and return the twenty to my pocket. "Thanks, Grandpa. I appreciate it."

He flips me off, then disappears into the kitchen.

I walk out of the dark bar and into the murky gray, cold rain drizzling from eaves above the entrance.

I wrap my coat around me as I rush to my car.

I hop in, turn on the heat, and catch a glimpse of something dark in my rearview, moving in the back seat.

I spin around, heart racing, body tensed, prepared for attack.

But there's nothing there.

Only a sense of overwhelming dread I can't place, and a warning voice inside me.

Something terrible is about to happen.

TWELVE

Delaney

It's the nicest area in Barton, but Westwood always feels lifeless and sterile.

Jay's apartment is in the heart of the shiny new metropolis that rose from the ashes, quite literally, of what was a working class immigrant area packed with Italians, Greeks, Russians, and Jews. Thanks to a blend of too many wildfires in too short a time — a suspicious amount, you might even say — and business interests, much of the area was gobbled up by eminent domain and rebuilt into a place its original residents could no longer afford.

The north side lost much of its charm and local flavor, especially when it came to the mom-and-pops and family-owned restaurants. Those businesses were starved out of existence so new chic places could bloom in their stead — larger, prettier, with a sheen of wealth and bland charm that cemented the city's new identity as the It Spot for tech startups in the northwest.

Revitalization worked for much of the community. Big and beautiful, where both people and businesses were clamoring to get in. Barton became the place to be, but it also lost its heart, and priced previous generations out of the future. Even those who hadn't lost their homes to eminent domain couldn't keep up with the skyrocketing property values and were eventually forced to sell.

Sure, many of them made a killing in the sale, but they'd lost their place in the world. The city lost its sense of community, replaced by people without any history or ties, attracted to the trendiest spot on the map.

But community and history rarely pays the bills or paves the way for progress. So life went on, the change holding its space as the only constant.

Jay's apartment is in a twenty-five-story building with unreasonable rent and an arresting view of the city and typically glittering bay.

I park in the garage using Jay's card, use the key his mother gave me to bypass the doorman downstairs, then take the elevator to the 29th floor.

If there was ever police tape on the door, it's gone now.

The apartment is still a mess, no doubt tossed by Rufus or his people searching for drugs. Shelves overturned, furniture torn open and foam everywhere. Every drawer emptied from every dresser. I'm glad his stuff is still here.

People's possessions often hold residual memories. The more personal an item, the more feelings or memories I can glean from holding them. I can't always pick up what I need, but it's easier than entering an empty room. The walls rarely remember as much.

Typically the landlord would've had the place cleaned out, but Jay's parents are still paying rent, and he's technically only missing. The apartment stays as is for now.

I walk slowly from room to room, ignoring the scenic view and waiting for something to whisper to me. Nothing in the living room, so I move to his bedroom. It's nice, or was. Cool and gray, minimalist.

The mattress is stripped and torn open, but I can feel something from it.

I touch the mattress and close my eyes.

A vision of Jay with a young blonde and many passionate exchanges.

A name — *Anika*.

The girlfriend.

I get visuals from Jay's perspective, some arousing since when I tap into a memory, I feel some bit of what the person was experiencing at the time. I push the sensations out of my mind. I'm not here as a voyeur.

I go to the closet and see clothes in heaps. I pick up a well-worn black tee and get a rush of memories, different times he's slid the shirt on or off — glimpses of Jay returning home from a party, high as a cloud, sliding the shirt off halfway before collapsing on the bed; a time he put it on in a rush to leave; another when he paced a warehouse floor while waiting for someone, afraid he'd get busted by the cops.

Usually when I touch someone's possessions, I get a memory from the past and some feeling about their present — where they are or an emotion they're feeling.

But I feel nothing in Jay's present. Does it mean he's dead? Not necessarily, but I'd prefer to feel something, some sign that he's out there so I can find him and give his mother good news.

I sense something from the bathroom, followed by a chill.

I turn, swearing that the door just moved.

My heart races as I get closer, suddenly certain that someone is in there.

It is Jay?

One of Rufus's men?

I pull my gun from my holster and cautiously approach the door with it aimed. "Come out!"

No response.

I kick the door open and see a flash of darkness moving behind me in the mirror.

I spin around, but there's nothing.

Is my mind playing tricks or am I seeing a memory of something?

They vary in strength, from a slight recall or imagining to the unrelenting severity of a full-blown hallucination. That's only happened a couple of times, and it's never good when it does.

There's a strong energy I can feel pressing on my chest, into my skin. A sense of déjà vu. Maybe the memories are mixing with my own. Or this is reminding me of something from my past, long ago buried.

I'm only certain of one thing. Something happened here.

I need to get into the bathroom so I can try tapping into any possible memories.

I clear the room of any potential threats and return my gun to its holster.

I look back in the mirror at myself, not sure what I'm expecting to see.

Then a flash, Anika pressing against the bathroom door, holding it shut, crying as it shakes and rattles.

Jay on the other side banging and screaming. "Open the fucking door!"

I feel Anika's fear as if it's my own, tasting it as if I'm living within it.

It's not the first time he's scared her. Was he abusive? Hard to tell from this one memory.

I hear his voice screaming to let him in. Like a muffled echo.

He says something else, but it's already fading.

I go in and close the door, sealing myself in the bathroom, then close my eyes and touch the door.

Another, stronger flash.

"Where is it, Anika? What did you do?"

Nothing is coming.

I get up and look around the room. I see a small pink T-shirt on the ground.

I pick it up and get a memory of Anika in it.

Then I see her, clear as day, working at a diner.

I've been there before.

I get a cold chill as I leave the bathroom.

I look back inside.

A flash of memory, something violent in the tub. But then it's gone, taking the details with it.

I leave the apartment shaken, knowing only that I need to find Anika. She knows what happened, or at least more than she told the cops.

I step into the elevator and push the ground floor button.

A man rushes in before the door can close. A green fatigue jacket and a black baseball cap pulled low, disguising his face.

I spot a tattoo on his hand, a double lightning bolt, and before I can put move to my holster, the man has a knife at my gut.

He looks up at me with empty blue eyes. His teeth tiny and sharp. Voice low and to the point. "What were you doing in there?"

I don't break my gaze. If he wanted to stab me, he would've done that already. I hope.

"Looking for Jay Sutherland. His parents hired me to find him. I'm a private investigator."

His eyes are probing mine like he's trying to spot a lie, looking for a reason to gut me.

"Do you know where he is?"

"No. I'm looking for him too," the man says, his knife still at my stomach.

"You mind moving that?"

"As long as you keep your hands where I can see them."

I raise my hands to show I'm not going to reach for my piece, but I'm already considering my options if he attacks. I'd disarm him, then grab his head and bring his face crashing into my knee. Disable the man before he can hurt me.

He pulls the blade away. "You find anything in there?"

"No. You a friend, associate, or other?"

"Associate," he says matter-of-factly. "So, what's the next step in your search?"

"I don't know. Any suggestions?"

"Nope." He shrugs. "But when you do find him, tell him he needs to get right with Rufus or he's gonna wish he was dead."

"Rufus. Gotcha," I say with a sarcastic little grin I can't avoid, even though it's poking the bear.

The elevator dings and opens into the parking garage.

The man gets out and walks away, keeping his eyes on me, as if I might shoot him.

A black car with dark tinted windows pulls up behind the guy. He doesn't turn, he just reaches for the handle, eyes on me the entire time, then gets in and closes the door.

The car tears off.

The license plate is missing. I'll hit the databases later and see what info I can get on Rufus and his crew.

The car is gone and my heartbeat slowly returns to

normal, though my mind is racing with questions. Was this guy sitting on the apartment, waiting for someone to show up or maybe for Jay to return? Or had he been watching Jay's mom? And if so, how long had he been following me? More importantly, why hadn't I felt the tail?

My senses are better than this.

I thought I'd seen something in my back seat. It hadn't been the man, I'm certain of that. Nothing about him felt supernatural. There's a fair amount of that in this city, but I didn't sense anything beyond normal street dealer from the guy.

But something is close and unsettling, teasing the edge of my memory.

Again, that foreboding certainty that something awful is about to happen. And that it somehow involves Anika.

I reach into my coat and touch her shirt. I close my eyes and see her at the diner. I think she's there now, though sometimes I get memories and visions confused.

Either way, it's time to pay Anika a visit.

THIRTEEN

Anika

Anika wakes at noon to her ringing phone. Surprisingly, she doesn't feel like shit from last night's pill.

She sees Ken's name and considers putting the phone down, but she takes it out of habit.

"I know it's your day off." He sounds so apologetic, she can't help but hear him out.

He's in the weeds. Margot is the only server who showed up. She's new, and Anika is his only reliable person. He'll owe her if she helps him.

Anika wishes he would value her enough to do something about her never getting good tables whenever Jolene and Candi screw her over. She's never said much to him, hoping he'd notice. Going behind a coworker's back usually has a way of getting out. It's difficult enough to work with people she doesn't like. The ones who actively hate her make everything miserable. But Ken's clueless about the people under his nose, even if he's otherwise smart.

Very smart, actually.

Anika has an idea.

She knows Ken likes her. He lives alone and has a decent chunk of money. He's always bragging about his frugality and investments. He's saving so he'll never have to work a day past forty. She's heard enough to know he could easily lend her fifteen grand.

She hates the idea of asking anyone for anything, especially something so big, but maybe he'd lend it to her. And, if she could get more tables at work, she could pay him back faster. Helping him out today could go a long way to ensuring that he see her true value, and maybe end the bullshit with Candi and Jolene.

She wouldn't lead him on, but she could use some of his interest. As long as she doesn't explicitly make him think he'll get anything in return, and she pays him back in full, there really isn't any harm.

"Okay, but yes, you do owe me."

"Thanks," he says, sounding relieved and grateful.

Anika drives to work in the rain, surprisingly confident that she might have found a solution to her Rufus problem.

She spends the first hour of the shift racing around and trying to handle her customers while also helping Margot to fix her multiple errors.

She's a young 18-year-old brunette with big glasses that make her face seem even smaller than it already does. She's painfully shy, and customers ask her to repeat herself all the time.

As Anika is returning from the kitchen with an order for a four-top she spots Margot behind the wall leading into the dining area, crying.

"What's wrong?" Anika asks, balancing her tray of food carefully.

"I messed up this guy's order and he reamed me out, called me a fucking idiot and a child, and now he's talking to Ken. I shouldn't cry, but … I dunno, I've just never had anyone yell at me like that."

"It's okay," Anika says, even though a part of her is thinking that Margot's way too soft for the high-stress environment of a restaurant like this. She'll need to toughen up.

"We've all been there. Don't worry, Ken'll take care of it."

"He's probably gonna fire me."

Anika laughs. "Right now you're better than half the other servers. You show up and you're reliable. That's big with Ken. Don't worry. Like I said, we've all been there."

Anika would hug her, but she can't do so without dropping her tray. "Go freshen up, I'll cover your tables."

"Thank you," Margot says, then goes to the bathroom.

Anika delivers the food to her four-top while Ken appeases the asshole customer who yelled at Margot with a comped meal and apologies.

He's a fat pale guy in his forties with black hair and a big black beard, and a too-tight red tee with a cartoon eagle holding a gun in one hand and a giant flag in the other. He's sitting next to a woman who looks like she's probably his wife but regretting the vow.

"Thank you," the man nods. "Glad to see that *someone* here knows how to do their job."

Ken continues to kiss his ass, even though the guy's attitude is entitled and arrogant. Even though he got his way and, presumably, the right meal in the end, he's acting damaged.

"I understand, sir, and I promise I'll talk to her. You're right, this is unacceptable."

She's new, for Christ's sake. Hell, even the best servers mess up every now and then.

Just once Anika would love to see Ken stand up for his

crew, but he's too much of a company man to risk angering the customer and endangering his job.

As Ken leaves the guy at the table, the man turns to his likely wife and laughs. Under his breath he says, "Told you we'd get a free meal."

Anika carries her empty tray past the couple and gives them a dirty look, then approaches Ken at one of the computers where he's processing the bill. "Hey, Ken?"

"Yeah?"

"I just heard that guy say to his wife 'told you we'd get a free meal.'"

Ken stares at her, eyebrows arched. "Really?"

"Yeah, so whatever he said Margot messed up, she probably didn't."

He shakes his head with a look of disappointment. "Thank you."

Anika wonders if he'll tell the guy to get the hell out or make him pay. She lingers, watching as Ken approaches the table, hoping to see him let loose on the man and his wife.

But he simply hands them the check, presumably paid in full, smiles, and issues another apology.

Business finally slows enough that Anika goes to watch the hostess station. As she stands there folding forks, knives, and spoons into cloth napkins, Ken approaches her.

"Thanks again for coming in, and for telling me about those scammers."

"What happened? Did they know you were onto them?"

"It wasn't worth it. Not with a guy like that. Sometimes you have to eat some crap in this business."

Anika nods. "Yeah. I get you."

It seems like he's working up the nerve to make conversation. Ken's not the kind of manager to use his position inappropriately. A nice guy with little game. The kind who will either die alone or, maybe make someone a loyal husband and doting father to their child. This world has a way of chewing up nice people, so the odds of alone forever are a safe bet.

"So, what *were* you going to do on your day off?" He ends with an uncomfortable laugh.

ASK HIM NOW. ASK HIM!

"Get some rest and recover from this cold."

"I'm sorry. Shelly said she'll come in at two, so if you wanna go then you can."

ASK HIM NOW! YOU HAVE HIS SYMPATHY. ASK HIM!

"I was wondering if—"

Anika is cut off as the front doors open and a group of a dozen or so shuffles in.

"Welcome to Paddy's Ale House," she greets them.

Ken welcomes one of the men in the group, an older man in a gray suit, as though he's someone important, and asks Anika to help him push three tables together for a large party.

She helps him, cursing herself for waiting. She might not get another chance.

Just as she finishes taking drink orders, another large party enters and Margot takes them. Anika hopes she can handle the group. She'll be too busy to help.

Ken, now acting as host, sits a woman in the farthest booth in the back of her section.

Anika approaches the woman and gets a strange vibe she can't place. The woman is in her late twenties. Pretty, with long dark hair and a strong look. Anika's not sure if it's the woman's jaw that makes her look so tough, or something else.

The woman looks up and her green eyes meet Anika's, filling her with the strongest sense of déjà vu.

"Do I know you?" Anika asks.

"I don't think so," says the woman, tilting her head slightly askew.

And, for a reason Anika can't understand, especially since she doesn't remember the woman and rarely forgets a face, she's sure that the woman is lying.

FOURTEEN

Delaney

"I don't think so," I say, feigning confusion.

There's something off about Anika, something I can't quite grasp, though I feel like I should get it in the way I intuitively understand most people. I can usually pick up on things they're feeling or grab a random flash of their thoughts. It's nothing I can follow, so it's not especially useful. I might pick up someone thinking about a book, but I can't dive deeper into the thought to see a title.

But with Anika, something is in the way.

No stray thoughts, or any emotions whatsoever.

"Weird. You look familiar."

"Maybe you've seen my porn," I joke.

Her face flushes before she realizes I'm kidding. She laughs, then asks if I want a drink.

I order a beer.

Sure, it'll be my second — or is it third? — of the morning.

I'm not hungry after the onion rings, but I can't just sit in her booth and not eat or it'll seem sketchy. I study the menu, looking for something to pick at while working Anika.

She brings my beer, still trying to figure me out. Maybe she's seen me on the news after I found that girl, but something tells me that's not it. There's a familiarity about her. Not just because I have her shirt in my pocket and some of Jay's memories in my head.

"Are you ready to order?"

"I'm having trouble deciding. So many choices. You have any suggestions?" I meet her eyes.

She's still looking at me like a puzzle to solve. "Can't go wrong with the bacon cheeseburger."

"Okay, then I'll have that."

"What do you want for a side? We've got French fries, sweet potato fries, onion straws, or our vegetable of the day."

"Fries will be fine. Thank you."

As she goes to put my order in, I take a drink. The beer is neither as cold or as good as the brew at Dusty's. I check my email on my phone, looking for potential clients, finding only spam and updates from my ignored social media accounts.

A text message pops up with a preview. Gerard.

Hey, I'm sorry about last night. Can we talk?

I leave it unread so he won't know I'm ignoring him. I don't have time for this.

I let out a sigh.

"You okay?" Anika surprises me, as I didn't even hear her approach. She's holding another beer.

This is the opening I was looking for. "Clingy boyfriend."

"Oh. Sorry."

Anika sets the beer down, looks like she might walk away.

"Can I ask you something?"

"Okay." She folds one hand over the other in front of her stomach. Defensive posturing. She doesn't trust me. I'll work on being more vulnerable, or at least playing the role.

"Is it wrong to go out with a guy but not let him sleep over?"

She looks surprised, relaxes a bit and unfolds her hands. "How long have you been dating?"

"I dunno," I laugh. "Six months?"

She leans forward, talking in a low voice even though there's nobody close enough to hear. "You're sleeping with him?"

"Oh, yeah, all the time. Just not *sleeping* with him. I like my space. I'm restless when there's someone next to me. When we're done, I want him gone, but he's like a chick, I swear, wants to cuddle and drift off together. After sex, I need to be alone in my bed. Is that weird?"

"Not at all. I like waking up next to someone, but I can definitely understand it."

"Is your boyfriend clingy?" I grasp at the opportunity, though maybe I should've been less obvious. "Or am I the only one with a girlfriend for a boyfriend?"

"I'm not with anyone right now," she says, hands back in front of her.

I'm losing her. I need to back off, not ask questions about Jay. Play it cool and get back to my guy.

"Well, count yourself lucky. I'm thinking I should break things off, but …" now I lean forward and whisper, "he's really good in bed."

She laughs. "Well, that *would* make it harder to say goodbye."

"I don't know what it is. I hear all my girlfriends whine about how their guy fucks them then wants to go play video games or something. I would kill for a guy like that.

I've got Cuddles the Needy Little Puppy. At least he's potty trained."

She laughs again. "Wow."

"Sorry, I don't mean to annoy you."

"No, you're good. Let me go check on your food."

"Thanks."

I try to think of a way to ask about Jay while I'm waiting, but nothing comes to me as she delivers my burger and fries, setting them in front of me.

"Do you love him?" Anika asks before she leaves, almost abruptly.

The question surprises me.

My answer surprises me more. "I ... I don't know."

"That's probably why you don't want him to sleep over. But what do I know? My last relationship was toxic. I should've kicked him out."

Finally, an opening!

"Did he hurt you?"

Anika nods.

I tell her a partial lie. "I used to live with a guy who was violent. Never thought I'd fall for a guy like that. It was always someone else — a friend, a loved one who couldn't see the abuse for what it was. It's never us, until it is."

Her eyes are welling up.

I push more, gently. "Whatever happened, it's not your fault."

Anika's eyes are wet and as her guard lets down, emotions are wafting off of her — fear, but also love and ... loss.

She's about to say something when another waitress approaches. "Can you help me? I messed up a bill and the computer's not letting me adjust it."

Anika wipes at her eyes, then gives me a smile and leaves.

Damn it.

How do I get back without seeming pushy?

I eat my burger. It's bathed in salt, as are the fries, typical of a chain, but whatever. I'm not hungry.

I keep waiting for Anika to come back, not just to resume the conversation, but to get me a Coke. She's working another table and almost seems like she's trying to avoid looking my way.

I scared her off.

She finally returns. I'm done with my food and am about to ask for a Coke, when she hands me my check.

"I'm off now, so Margot can take care of this for you."

She hurries away, never even giving me a chance to stop her.

FIFTEEN

Anika

Anika is shaken by the woman in the booth, so oddly familiar, and a bit too curious about her relationship with Jay.

She feels like a cop, and the voice is warning her. The woman is not to be trusted. She takes Ken up on his offer and clocks out. But she asks to speak with him alone before going.

There's only one chair in his small, cluttered office. So Anika stands.

"What is it?" he asks.

She's still not sure how much to tell him. Too much and he'll probably suggest that she talk to the cops. Not enough and he'll miss the urgency of her request.

"Ken, I need to ask you for a huge favor. I'm not sure how, so I'm just going to come right out with it."

"What's that?" He leans forward, his eyes friendly and receptive.

"I'm in a bit of a jam and need to borrow some money. A lot of money, more than anyone should ask to borrow, but I will pay you back as fast as I can."

"How much?"

His eyes widen when she tells him. After a long sigh he says, "I wish I could help you, Anika. But … and this isn't public knowledge, I've been struggling."

"*Struggling?* How?"

He looks down, then tells the floor about his gambling addiction in a muffled, muddled mumble that takes Anika several seconds to decipher.

She finally gets it and bites on her tongue to keep a serious face.

A gambling addiction?

From the guy who is always lecturing others on how to spend their money and save?

The guy who brags about his financial independence?

He's got a gambling problem?

Of course he does. She was stupid to think the solution would be this easy.

"Oh, I'm sorry."

"I wish I could help. What do you need it for? Maybe I can help you think of a way out."

"I doubt that," she says, helpless and stuck.

She has two options left — sell the necklace to a jeweler who appraised it a while back, or ask Chelsea, which Anika doesn't want to do because it means admitting all the things her sister has accused her of — dating losers, being self-destructive, and making stupid choices.

"Never mind. Thank you."

Anika rushes out of his office before he can ask more questions and before she breaks down.

She grabs her purse from her locker, the gun a heavy anchor inside it. Her purse is large, and there's no way to see the gun's bulge, but still she feels like everyone can see it.

She's not sure why it feels so wrong. It's protection. It's

not like she's planning to rob a bank or go on a shooting spree, yet she feels an almost incomprehensible shame.

Anika wonders if she can pull the trigger. Or will she freeze and have the gun taken away and used on her?

Her heart is racing, chest tight with terror that she'll walk outside and run into Rufus, demanding his money. He said three days, but maybe he's planning to pay her a friendly reminder.

She walks briskly through the dining room toward the front doors, avoiding eye contact from her coworkers and the woman with her questions.

Outside, she unzips her bag and slips her hand inside, gripping the gun, just in case. She wants to get home, take pills and forget.

She reaches her car, unlocks the door, and sinks into the seat, relieved to be alone.

She starts the car, reverses, and tears out from her spot, eager to put the restaurant in the rearview mirror. Drives hard, not ready to go home.

She's trying to think of a way to get money, circling back to her necklace.

Or talking to Chelsea.

Her sister might give her shit, but in the end, she'll understand. And she'll still help even if she doesn't. Because that's what family is for.

Anika thinks back to their time together with Ed and Judy. They were great foster parents and Chelsea was a good sister.

EXCEPT WHEN SHE WASN'T.

EXCEPT WHEN SHE LOOKED DOWN ON YOU.

Anika shakes her head, hating how much a part of her still envies Chelsea, hating her inability to let go of old grievances. She loves her sister, truly wants the best for her.

And yet, she has this anger for how Chelsea has treated

her at times over the years. Her disappointment when she overdosed. The way she yelled, telling Anika that she always found a way to fuck things up.

She was just scared. She loves me.

YEAH, BUT SHE ALSO LOOKS DOWN ON YOU. JUDGES YOU. SHE DIDN'T BELIEVE YOU ABOUT DR. CARMINE, MADE YOU DOUBT YOURSELF WHILE HE KEPT ABUSING YOU. SHE HAD IT EASIER THAN YOU. ALWAYS DID, AND YET ACTS LIKE SHE HAD IT ROUGHER, BUT SHE PULLED HERSELF UP BY HER BOOTSTRAPS WHILE YOU … WALLOWED IN YOUR SELF-PITY AND DRUG ABUSE. FACE IT, SHE THINKS YOU'RE A LOSER.

Maybe I am. I did make stupid decisions. Me doing drugs is my fault, nobody else's.

YOU WENT THROUGH HELL. WHAT ELSE COULD YOU DO? YOU'VE DONE WELL FOR YOURSELF. YOU GOT A JOB AND YOU PAY ALL YOUR BILLS. YEAH, YOU WENT OUT WITH A BAD GUY, BUT YOU DIDN'T KNOW IT. HE LIED, PRETENDED TO BE A GOOD MAN. NOT YOUR FAULT. YOU DIDN'T KNOW ANY BETTER.

Tears are streaming down Anika's cheeks. It's all she can do not to turn the car around, head home, and swallow some pills. But that would be another bad decision. She has to prove she's not that person anymore. Her past can't dictate her future. She can do the right thing.

And that means turning to family for help.

But halfway to Chelsea's, Anika realizes she might not be home.

She calls and gets her sister's voicemail.

"Hi, Chelsea. It's Anika. Sorry about flaking out on you. Can we talk? I'm in your neighborhood."

She hangs up and keeps driving as it starts to rain again.

Anika doesn't see her sister's car. It might be in the garage. But maybe she isn't home.

She looks at her phone to see if Chelsea has called back. No.

She pulls up to the house as rain pelts her roof and windows. She picks up the phone and calls again, but still no answer.

Anika gets out of the car and walks up to the front door, looks through the window but doesn't see anyone in the living room.

SHE'S NOT HERE. JUST GO.

She rings the bell.

No answer.

She rings again.

Still nothing.

She runs back to her car, slipping and falling hard on her ass, soaking her clothes, pain shooting through her ass and back.

Damn it!

Anika stands, carefully, and gets in her car, slams the door and starts the engine.

She backs up.

As she does, she sees the blinds to one of the rooms in the house move.

Anika stops the car, staring, unsure if she really saw movement.

The blinds are still.

THEY WERE OPEN WHEN YOU WALKED UP. REMEMBER?

She can't remember.

Chelsea IS HOME AND IGNORING YOU.

Why would she do that?

BECAUSE SHE DOESN'T CARE ABOUT YOU.

SHE KNOWS YOU'RE JEALOUS.

SHE'S DISAPPOINTED IN YOU.

YOU'RE A BURDEN, THE ONE BAD THING IN HER LIFE, THE ONE THING SHE WISHES SHE COULD FORGET. YOU ARE ALWAYS IN THE WAY.

Anika heads home, feeling more alone than ever, craving the only thing that's ever helped.

SIXTEEN

Delaney

I'm sitting in my car across the street from Anika's apartment complex as the rain pours down.

She left work in such a hurry, I almost failed to trail her.

But then I followed her to a house that turns out to be her foster sister's place. She fell and now it looks like she might be having a breakdown. I want to help, but she doesn't know or trust me.

I'll need to think up some other ruse to gain her faith. Maybe go back to the diner and get her section again, initiate a conversation. Try not to spook her this time.

I almost always know the right way to earn a person's trust. It's served me well over the years, and I've never felt guilty because I'm usually manipulating liars. I'm not sure what kind of liar Anika is, but she's hiding something for sure.

She was dating a drug dealer, so she lives in a world of moral grays to survive. She lies to cover for him. Maybe to herself because there's no other way to exist in that world.

She's probably hiding his whereabouts — assuming he's alive. And that's far from a given.

She's throwing me off my game. On the rare occasions I use the wrong approach or my lead clams up, I can leverage something else against them. But I still have nothing with Anika.

I'd generally chalk this up to asshole got murdered by the people he ripped off, but Rufus wouldn't have his people on Jay's apartment if that was it.

Could be a rival gang.

I head downtown, find some of the places the other dealers hang out, and see what I can find.

My phone rings.

The caller? Morning Sun.

A tightening in my gut. Something's wrong. My father is dead.

I answer, expecting a doctor to deliver the news.

"Del?"

Father *never* calls. His voice is tinged in a sorrow I'm not sure I've heard from him before.

"Is everything okay?"

"Are *you* okay, Del?"

"I'm fine. Why?"

"We need to talk. Can you visit?"

"I'm in the middle of a case and—"

"It's important, Del. Please. Come now."

"Now?"

"I'm not sure how long I'll be … clear."

His voice is unsettling. It's the clarity, which I've not heard in years, with a vulnerability glazing the top. My father sounds afraid.

"I'm on my way."

~

I SEE my father in the dining area, sitting alone, dressed for a reservation in his nicest gray jacket and pants. His nurse, Rosita, approaches me.

"Hi, Del, how are you?" She gives me a hug.

"Good, you?"

"Okay," she says, smiling. "Your dad is doing so well today. I haven't seen him like this ... ever. And he seems almost desperate to get ahold of you."

"That's even rarer," I tease. "What's it about?"

"I don't know, but he keeps asking if you're here yet. So, you better not keep him waiting."

"Thanks," I say and head into the dining area as Rosita heads the other way.

He smiles when he sees me, almost shockingly alert. He looks ten years younger, maybe more. He's still in a wheelchair, but it looks like he could probably push himself out of it.

I sit across from him. We don't do hugs, and am surprised to see him still looking at me with a smile. I wonder about his meds.

"How are you?"

"Fine." His voice is neither frail nor weak. "I just needed to see you."

"What did you want to talk about?"

"I saw Brother Clarence."

"Who?" I ask before remembering his right-hand man. Clarence is older than Father by at least twenty years, so the dude must be ancient. I haven't seen him since Father lost the church and went to prison. Last I heard he was back in Alabama or something.

"Brother Clarence. You remember him, don't you?" He's smiling like his long-lost best friend had just come home. Maybe he had.

"Where did you see him?"

He points to his head. "Up here."

"Um, what?"

"I saw him up here when I woke up. He's coming to visit."

His smile is so earnest I don't have the heart to tell him that he's imagining things, that Brother Clarence will not be visiting. Maybe he'll forget in twenty minutes and his heart will be spared.

Dementia has its benefits.

Suddenly Father is telling stories about how he and Clarence went door-to-door in the early days, spreading the gospel and building the church one nonbeliever at a time. Most folks didn't trust Clarence because he was the blackest man any of them had ever seen. Still, he had a way of winning people over and was the beating heart of their church.

"It was Clarence who saw your gifts first, you know? Who recognized your talents."

"I remember it differently," I say, settling into our oldest argument.

He waves a hand dismissively. "You never had gratitude for your gifts. Most people would've killed for a kiss from God."

"Yeah, all the good it's doing me. I haven't been able to heal anyone since I was a kid. I can't even heal my own father."

"But you have other gifts now. You … find people. You found that missing girl."

I'm surprised he heard about it. I never told him. He was too out of it and it didn't matter, anyway.

"Never question the blessing. Just accept it. Be grateful."

"It's hard to be grateful with this. I can't use it to find the people I want to find."

He looks down. He knows who I'm talking about.

Old wounds are reopening. I want to lash out. "Since we're strolling down Memory Lane and you're remembering stuff, maybe you can tell me where my mom went."

"You're the last person she reached out to, not me."

"A postcard from France is hardly reaching out."

"It's more than I ever got." He sounds wounded. His smile is gone. I bet he regrets calling me. I hope he does.

"Well, whose fault is that? Clearly you did something to make her miserable, to make her leave. Let's cut the shit. Neither of us is getting any younger, and hell, I don't know the next time you'll have your memories back, if ever."

He flinches. That hurt.

Good. It doesn't even start to pay him back for all the pain he's given me.

"What did you do to make her leave?"

"I told you, I don't know. I thought she was happy."

"She was always crying!"

"No she wasn't."

"How would you even know? You were either working at the church or out God knows where at all hours, supposedly helping people. But you were never home, and come on, we both know the truth. You were cheating and she found out, right?"

"I was *never* unfaithful. I loved your mother with all my heart." His eyes are watering and now I feel like shit for pushing too hard. He deserves to suffer, not only for what he did to me, exploiting my 'power' for his benefit, but also for all the people he bilked out of money before getting caught. Still, he doesn't deserve to have Mother used against him this way.

"I'm sorry." I swallow the word like a stone.

He looks at me for a long time with a trembling lip. I

don't know if it's anger or some symptom of his disease. Maybe he's about to forget everything, including who I am.

He finds his words. "You think you're the victim in all this. You live your life like some tragedy, but you have no idea … no idea what you put us all through."

"What?" I ask, bewildered and pissed. "What I put *you all* through? I'm sorry, I didn't ask to be put on some pedestal and used—"

Father's no longer listening to me.

He's looking up, past me.

His eyes are wide.

I turn around.

It's Brother Clarence, the giant man in a black suit, even darker skin, and the brightest golden eyes I've ever seen. He doesn't appear a day older than the last time I saw him more than a decade ago.

"Hello, Delaney." He's holding a black bowler hat in his big hands, and nodding at me.

SEVENTEEN

Anika

Where are they?

Anika's heart is racing, her mind ablaze and spiraling out of control. Panic on full blast. Brutal waves rushing at her crumbling shore over and over, threatening to drag her into the dark, dark sea.

She needs her pills.

She's torn the apartment apart and can't find them anywhere.

She's pacing her bedroom, bed tossed, nightstand drawer out with its contents spilled onto the floor. She's checked all her clothes, behind the bed and in her car. Everywhere else she remembers having the baggie.

They're gone.

And her sanity with them.

Did I take them all and forget?

Did I drop them somewhere?

Did someone break in and take them?

A thud pulls her attention toward her door.

Is someone out there?

Are they coming for me?

She approaches it slowly, then peers through the eyehole.

Nobody in front of her door, but … is something moving in the corner? The area near the stairwell seems unnaturally dark, like someone broke the light to create a patch of shadows to hide in. And wait.

She shakes her head, trying to clear the anxiety, but her hands are shaking. She can't help but feel like her world is about to spilt at the seams, or, maybe crash in on her.

She was so good this morning, and now she can't function. She needs more pills.

As she's tearing through her clothes in one last hope that they'll spill out, she finds Frankie's phone number.

I probably shouldn't. Frankie has to be the one who sold me out to Rufus.

WELL, RUFUS ALREADY FOUND YOU. DAMAGE DONE. NO HARM IN GETTING SOMETHING YOU OBVIOUSLY NEED.

Anika calls without hesitation.

"Who's this?" he asks.

Anika is about to say her name, but instead says, "Big Jay's girl."

"You wanna take me up on my offer?"

"Yes," she says, figuring he's probably asking if she needs a refill but isn't about to say so on the phone. She isn't even sure if cops listen. Jay never acted afraid.

"Where you at?"

"I'm leaving a friend's house," Anika lies. "Where can we meet?"

"I'm on the south side, running errands. How about that bookstore in the new Agora? Grab a book or a coffee and hang out near the cafe. I'll find you."

"Okay," she says.

He's already hung up.

This is a mistake. Her heart is racing faster, nervous thoughts multiplying.

WHAT THE HELL ARE YOU DOING?

WHAT IF COPS BUST YOU?

WHAT IF HE TRIES TO HURT YOU?

WHAT IF RUFUS IS WAITING WITH HIM?

She should cancel. Every fiber of Anika's logical brain is telling her to, but that other part is already grabbing the keys and shoving her out the door.

ANIKA IS IN A BROOKES & Taylor Bookstore, sitting in an oversized orange loveseat with a latte and a hardcover she grabbed from a table in the front of the shop, *A Hardship for Elise.*

She has no idea what the book is about, despite having read the blurb and the first few pages at least five times.

She can't focus on anything but the front doors, waiting for Frankie.

He didn't say when he'd be there, but she assumed he'd meet her right away. It's taking forever. She wants to call him, but not enough to seem overeager. Anika also doesn't want to tip off any cops who might be listening on Frankie's line.

OR YOURS.

Why would they be tapping my line?

WHY WAS THAT COP SNOOPING AROUND? MAYBE THEY THINK YOU HAD SOMETHING TO DO WITH JAY'S DISAPPEARANCE.

Her chest is tight. A cold sweat beads down her back. She has that feeling again, like the walls are closing in. The noose is tightening, and she's half-dead already.

Anika stands, leaving her book on the seat to make a beeline for the front door.

Screw the pills. She's going home.

She gets into her car and hits the ignition.

Her phone rings with an unknown number.

She answers. "Hello?"

"Yeah, sorry, my car died. Got a ride home from a friend. You wanna swing by my place?"

No, she doesn't.

But then he says, "I'm like a five-minute drive from you."

This is a mistake. But her heart is racing fast and Anika's afraid if she doesn't get something to calm her nerves she might have a heart attack and die.

"Where are you at?"

Frankie tells her.

~

ANIKA FEELS like an interloper looking for Frankie's address in the heart of the south side's ghetto. The rain is gone, but the skies are still overcast.

She's not used to this part of town. The kind of place that's on the news every night. Gunfights, gang wars, drug busts, robberies, domestic disputes turned violent, rape, you name it. Most of Barton's crimes are in this neighborhood, an impoverished three-square-mile chunk of the city with high unemployment and hope that lives in the gutters. Government housing and shuttered businesses. The few remaining shops look like fortresses. Iron bars on their windows and doors, moats of despair in crumbled concrete all around them.

She passes a group of young black men standing

around a Supra, rap thumping through the car's metal doors and into her bones.

They look at her suspiciously as she passes. She glances away, not wanting to provoke them.

She feels a flush of guilt for assuming they mean her harm. Anika's never considered herself remotely close to racist. She's looked up to Chelsea for most of her life. Anika's fear is borne from the deep poverty and sinking desperation. Distressed people do dangerous things. She'd seen enough of that seedy underworld when she dated Jay to know what areas and people were most dangerous.

Anika tells herself that she'd feel just as afraid of young white men glaring at her. Any man in a place like this. Maybe some of the women.

She slows to a crawl as the addresses get close to the one she's looking for. Frankie's place is a garishly-painted blue duplex in the ghetto, situated between two similar duplexes, one pink and the other green. The pink one appears vacant. The green one has six cars in front of the house and a pit bull chained up out front.

All three duplexes, and most of the surrounding houses, are covered in bars.

Anika parks, gripping the gun in her purse. She gets out of the car, locks it, then rushes to the front door as the pit bull starts to snarl and bark at her.

She knocks on the red paint-flaked door.

She hears movement on the other side, then several locks sliding open.

Frankie cracks the door, looks her up and down, then past her, like he's expecting Anika to have brought friends. Seeing no one else, he nods her inside.

She enters the dark, small living room. He closes the door and locks it.

Blue light bleeds from the apartment's only bedroom, the sound of a movie on a TV.

"Back here." He leads her to the room.

Anika keeps her hand on the gun. He looks a bit high, so maybe he doesn't notice. The place reeks of weed.

His bedroom is even smaller than Anika expected, with a king-size occupying most of the space. A 50-something-inch TV sits on a dresser, the room's only other furniture.

He sits on the bed, scoots over, patting it for Anika to sit beside him. He's cross-legged, rolling a joint from a giant bag of weed. There are several large white pill bottles beside it, along with an army of plastic baggies. Apparently, this is where Frankie prepares his drugs for sale.

She stares at the spot, hoping he doesn't have the wrong idea.

He shakes his head and rolls his eyes. "Chillax, girl. I'm not gonna do anything to you."

She sits, but can't keep her hand on the gun without drawing attention, so she sets her purse on the ground beside the bed. It's unzipped. If Frankie does anything, she'll dive for it, then turn around and fire.

He laughs at the movie, and she recognizes it as *Groundhog Day*.

He lights a joint, takes a deep drag, then offers it to her.

She shakes her head. "No thanks."

"Ah, just a pill girl, eh? I feel ya. So, whatcha need?"

He lifts each bottle, shakes it as he names the pills, then drops each one back to the bed.

She chooses the painkillers she's always taken.

"How many you need?"

She doesn't want to say a lot and seem like an addict. But she also doesn't want to come back. Not ever again. She just needs enough to get through this rough patch.

"I dunno, what do people normally get?"

He laughs as takes another drag. "You get whatever you want. How about sixty? That'll do you?"

She nods.

He tells her the price, steeper than she expected.

"How about thirty?"

He halves the total.

She digs into her purse, grabs the cash and hands it to him.

"Hold up." Frankie hops up and off the bed, sprints out of the room, then returns with a cold bottle of water before launching himself back on the bed. He plops down, untwists the cap, then hands it to Anika.

"What?"

"I need you to take one now."

"Now?"

"Just gotta make sure you're actually gonna use them. That you're not a narc."

"I'm not a narc."

"Be glad I didn't strip search you. Now take the pill or get the fuck out."

"But I need to drive back home."

"One pill ain't gonna fuck you up that bad."

She stares at the bottle in his hand, then at the one on his bed. Thirty pills, or even twenty-nine, would go an awful long way to calming her down.

She takes the bottle, accidentally splashing cold water on her hand.

He gives her a pill and she takes it, follows with a swig of water, then nods as she hands the bottle back to Frankie.

"See, not so bad." He screws the cap back on and drops the water in front of him.

He starts counting pills into a smaller bottle.

His phone rings and he loses count.

"Sorry," he says, taking the call and talking to one of his crew about stupid shit.

She needs to get the hell out, but tries to relax and enjoy the buzz from the pill while watching Bill Murray.

Frankie tells her to hang tight, then leaves her to take the call outside. He's on the phone for what feels like forever. Anika eyes the pill bottles and wonders if she could steal some without him noticing. Maybe, but the idea of him searching her on the way out is terrifying.

She focuses on the movie to stave the temptation. Every now and then she hears Frankie's voice over the TV, yelling about some asshole or "punk-ass bitch."

She's not sure why, but hearing him say "punk-ass bitch" is much funnier than it should be.

She's cracking up by the time he finally returns.

And she's incredibly tired.

Too tired.

Something is wrong.

She tries to get up, but is too dizzy.

What's wrong? Did he drug me?

Anika tries to get up again but instead she falls to the bed.

EIGHTEEN

Delaney

"Brother Clarence." I stand, surprised to see him, and shocked to see that he still looks exactly the same. How is that possible?

"It's so good to see you both." He nods. Never a smile from him, always so serious.

He passes me, maybe remembering I'm not a hugger, and takes a seat next to Father, clasping his hands. "Hello, old friend."

"Hello," Father says, tears welling up in his eyes.

I don't think he's ever shown even a fraction of such joy to see me.

I sit beside them.

Father asks Brother Clarence how his trip was and how he's been. They're making small talk while I'm trying to sort out how he knew Brother Clarence was coming and how the hell the man can look so young.

Does Dad have a psychic gift similar to mine? Can he sometimes see things before they happen? Or is he somehow connected to Brother Clarence?

I was the only gifted one in our family, so far as I know.

If Father's also gifted, why not tell me? Unless there's some other explanation.

"What brings you here, Brother Clarence?"

It feels like his golden eyes can see right through me, into my thoughts. I realize that Brother Clarence is the one with a gift.

"I came because the end is near."

"What do you mean?"

Brother looks at Father. "Did you not tell her?"

He shakes his head.

"What is it?" I ask.

Father meets my eyes. His tears are gone. Matter-of-factly he says, "I'm dying."

"What do you mean? The nurse didn't say anything."

"They don't know."

"Wait, then how do *you* know?"

He nods at Brother Clarence. "He told me. In a dream."

I laugh, but then see Brother not laughing.

"What are you talking about?"

"Your father will die soon. I've come to make peace and forgive him."

"What do you mean he's dying? Of what?"

"I only know he will be gone soon."

"I don't know what the hell is going on here, or what kind of shit you told him, but you'd better start making sense or I'm getting security to escort your ass out of here."

"Delaney!" Father yells, glaring at me.

"It's okay." Brother Clarence is either ignoring or blissfully unaware of my brewing rage. "She is right to be wary." He studies me before frowning. "You've not told her anything, have you?"

Father shakes his head sharply, trying to silence the man.

"Told me what?"

Brother looks at me. "I need a word with your father. Could you give us a few minutes?"

"Anything you have to say to him you can say in front of me. I'm his custodian."

"Delaney!" Father is so loud and sharp, I'm suddenly a kid and his voice has terrified me into obedience.

I stand and say, "Five minutes."

I leave them be, heading back to the front desk.

Nancy's on the phone while reading one of her "spicy romance" novels.

She looks up from her book before putting it down. "Hey, girl, how are you?"

"I don't want to interrupt."

"You ain't interrupting a damned thing. These fools think I've got all day to sit on hold."

"How's Keshawn?" I ask.

"He's alright. He moved closer to me. Got an apartment and everything. Said he's gonna give you some money for that car."

"It's not necessary, really. Business is picking up. But, I might have something he can help me with."

"What's that?"

I tell her a bit about the Big Jay situation and how I'm wondering if a rival dealer might've taken him out. Keshawn ran with a rough crew and might know something, or at least someone I can talk to without getting my ass shot.

Nancy looks at me for a long moment. "He ain't gonna snitch. He's turning his life around. He don't need that kind of heat."

"I wouldn't jam him up. I just need a general direction. Nobody will ever know we spoke."

She gives me his number and I put it in my phone. "Thanks, Nancy. I'll let you get back to your smut."

"It's spicy romance." She laughs.

"*Literary* spicy romance," I add.

"Yes!"

I go outside and make a quick call to Keshawn. I'm expecting to leave a message and am surprised when he answers.

"Keshawn?"

"Yeah. Is this that Del lady who gave me the Mustang?"

"Yes."

"I'm gonna send you some money. I feel bad. You know how much that thing is worth?"

"Well, it wasn't worth much until you fixed it. We're good. But I was hoping you could help me out with something."

"What you need?"

I tell him the situation, then ask if he knows anything about it or whom I might talk to.

Keshawn is quiet, but after a moment he says, "I don't hang around those guys anymore."

"I understand. It was a shot in the dark. Thanks, anyway."

"I might know who might know something, but you can't tell him I told you."

"Go on …"

"Guy named Skeezy."

"Skeezy?"

"Don't ask. Anyway, he knows all the shit going down. And he'll talk if you grease him."

"He won't think I'm a cop?"

"He's got a sixth sense for that stuff. Tell him straight up who you are and what you're doing. He'll help if the price is right. But he ain't cheap. I'm guessin' if these parents is as rich as you say, that won't be a problem."

"Where do I find this guy?"

Skeezy works at his brother's computer shop downtown and might go by Stanley at work. But I won't need to ask for either, as I'll know the guy when I see him.

Keshawn laughs when I ask what that means. "Oh, you'll see."

I say thanks, assure him that our conversation is sealed, then hang up and head back inside to get answers from my father and Brother Clarence.

I don't know what the hell is happening, but it's something big. Maybe it's even got to do with my mom disappearing.

Is she still alive?

Is that the secret they're keeping?

And if she is alive, why not tell me sooner?

I go back and find Father sitting alone in the restaurant, staring out the window, deep in thought. I take a seat and ask where Brother Clarence is.

He's startled, looking at me like I'm a stranger.

"Father?"

His brow furrows in confusion.

Shit. He's lost again.

He's staring, hands trembling.

I look around for Brother Clarence, but see only a handful of residents.

I head back toward the front, find Nancy back on the phone, calmly explaining to someone that no, exceptions cannot be made. If they would like to have a conversation with her boss, they are welcome to call her.

She hangs up and looks over, seeing my worry.

I ask her if she's seen Brother Clarence.

"Who?"

"The man who came to visit my father."

"Nobody else has come here for him today."

I describe Brother Clarence. No way she'd miss his height or his eyes.

She shakes her head. "I haven't seen anybody like that."

What the——?

I'M SITTING WITH FATHER, listening to him talk about an old TV show he used to watch, *Quincy*. He's been talking to me for fifteen minutes about old cases he's seen the detective solve. He can remember details of some damned mystery show from the 80s like he just watched it, but he can't remember his own daughter.

Maybe they show *Quincy* reruns here. He does watch a lot of TV.

Still, I can tell he has no idea who he's talking to, that he probably thinks I'm one of the people who works here.

I'm waiting in hopes that either Father comes back, or Brother Clarence does. Meanwhile, I'm sitting sideways with my phone on my lap where he can't see me checking email while he continues to drone on and on.

A message from Gerard: *Can I come by tonight?*

Ugh.

Can't tonight. With my father right now and it's been a rough day.

The ellipsis appears and sticks around. He's typing something super long. Then it suddenly goes away and I wonder if he paused or deleted what he wrote.

He finally replies. *Sorry. Anything I can help with?*

No. Sorry.

He reads the message and goes offline.

Okay, then.

At some point my father's stopped talking about Jack Klugman.

I look over to see him staring at me, head tilted, eyeing me intently. I'm hopeful he's back. "What is it?"

He's looking at and through me. "That girl has the devil in her."

"What? What girl?" I'm looking around, thinking maybe he was looking at one of the workers. Sometimes he says crazy shit and they've gotta bring his meds. "What girl has the devil in her?"

His eyes are locked on mine, and they're welling up with tears.

He reaches out and touches my hand, squeezing it tight.

"What girl has the devil in her?"

"Anika."

"What?"

"Don't go near her."

"What are you talking about?"

"Don't go near her, Delaney. It knows what you are."

"What are you talking about?"

Father is staring at me, then through me again. His head tilts and he looks at me, confused. "Were you saying something, ma'am?"

He's lost again.

And now, so am I.

NINETEEN

Anika (Age 13)

Anika is sitting on the couch across from her therapist, Dr. Carmine, nervous as he asks her to tell him what she remembers.

She doesn't like to talk about the things that happened before. Mostly because it's so hard to recall, but also because the few things she can still see when she closes her eyes hurt like a rotting tooth.

"I don't remember."

"We both know that's not true," he says from his chair opposite Anika. "As we discussed last time, you're safe here. You need a space to process the trauma or it will seep into other areas of your life. You understand how that works, right?"

Anika nods, looking at him. He has one leg crossed over the other. Anika's not sure why, but she can't stop staring at the exposed white hairless area between where his dark sock ends and his gray slacks begin.

He shifts in his chair, uncrossing his leg. She's sure he's spotted her looking.

Embarrassed, she pretends to stare at the floor before

meeting his gaze. He's chewing on the end of a pencil. He does that a lot.

He's good looking for an older, heavyset man. He's tall and has a kind face, blue eyes that remind Anika of her mom's.

She's been coming for a few months. It's been helping with the nightmares. She doesn't want to disappoint him by regressing.

"What do you want me to talk about?"

"Just tell me a bit about your parents."

"I've told you about them."

"Not everything," he says.

Anika tells him what she remembers, mostly little things. How her father used to be so sweet. He'd come home every Friday he got paid and bring her some little toy, book, or item of clothing. Nothing big. Just a little something to show he'd been thinking about her.

Anika tells him how her mom would always read to her at night. But not different books. She had to read the same one, over and over and over. If she suggested a new one, Anika would cry.

"Why do you think that was?" Dr. Carmine asks.

"I don't know. I just *really* liked the story?"

"What story was it?"

"*Percy the Unicorn*. Have you heard of it?"

"No."

Anika tells him what she remembers of the plot and finds herself feeling a warmth in her stomach as she remembers the story she hasn't heard in forever. She's surprised how much she remembers, especially when so much of her earliest life is fuzzy.

She wonders where the book is now. The house had burned down. Her mom's necklace is all she has left, but she would trade it for that copy of *Percy the Unicorn*.

Dr. Carmine says that sounds like a sweet story. He asks about her father, and what he said when drunk.

Anika tells him what she remembers, hating the way his words make her cry even now. She wonders if she's crying more for what he said or for the loss of the dad he could have been.

"Did he ever touch you?" Dr. Carmine asks.

"Hit me?"

He shifts in his seat, crosses his leg again. "No, did he *touch you?*"

Anika's still not sure what he means. Then it dawns on her.

"Oh … oh God, no."

"Good." Something in his voice is off. Like he's out of breath.

He asks Anika to talk about the night her mother died.

She doesn't remember much. So he asks about another night when her father hurt her mother. She tells him about the time he choked Mommy, then ripped Edwin's head off.

He stands and paces as she tells him. Anika's not sure why, but she can feel him looking at her every so often, though not even once does she look up or into his eyes.

Hot tears paint her cheeks as she remembers watching her father rip Edwin's head off. She loved him almost as much as she loved her mommy, back before he turned permanently mean.

"How did that make you feel when he did that?"

She cries harder, burying her face in her hands.

Dr. Carmine sits beside Anika and puts his arms around her.

The touch shocks her at first. She didn't think a doctor was supposed to touch you like that. But Anika needs a hug right now and someone to hear her crying.

So she trusts him.

TWENTY

Anika (Now)

WAKE UP, GIRL.
WAKE THE FUCK UP!
Heart like a hammer at her chest.
Eyes wide, alert, taking in the moment.
A strange bed, her shirt ripped. The bed is covered in blood. So is she.
No memory of where she is or how she got here.
Then she remembers.
Frankie!
He drugged her.
She dives down, reaches for the gun, and grabs it from her purse.
She sits up too quickly, blood rushing to her head. She's dizzy, looking for Frankie.
Blood is soaking through her clothes, the reek of it turns her stomach.
Anika thinks it's hers, but she's not cut, save for a few scratches she can feel on her face.
She approaches the open bedroom door, gun raised,

shaking in her hand as she peers into the living room and kitchen.

His apartment is empty. Rain is falling hard on the roof and windows.

Where is he?

COME ON. WE NEED TO GET THE HELL OUT OF HERE!

What happened?

NO TIME. GRAB THE DRUGS, LET'S GO.

She grabs the bottles from the nightstand, shoves the pills into her purse and stumbles forward.

WAIT.

WIPE DOWN ANYTHING YOU TOUCHED. REMOVE THE PRINTS.

Why? What happened to him? What did he do to me?

YOU KNOW WHAT HE DID TO US. AND WHAT WE HAD TO DO TO HIM.

No, she doesn't. But Anika obeys the inner voice. It's always guided her when she needed it most.

She only touched the water bottle.

TAKE IT.

She grabs it from the nightstand and shoves it in her purse.

LET'S GO!

She reaches for the door.

WAIT!

She pauses.

Hears music thumping from just outside. A car passing by.

It passes.

NOW!

She goes outside.

It's raining hard, meaning there's not as many people

hanging outside their homes. The sky is dark, though not yet nighttime.

She rushes to her car, hoping nobody happens to be looking out their window.

Yes, officer, I saw the girl and the car she was driving.

A dog barks and makes her jump. She looks next door to see the pit bull still chained to the tree. It barks louder when she looks at it.

Who leaves a dog in the rain?

She wishes she could free it, but it'd probably bite her.

She opens the car door.

GRAB THE BLANKET FROM THE BACK.

PUT IT ON THE SEAT SO THERE'S NO BLOOD.

She obeys, then gets in.

Anika puts the car in reverse, careful not to back out too fast and draw attention to herself.

She drives, keeping her head down, refusing to freak out, praying she won't see a cop's light bar flashing behind her.

She makes it out of the neighborhood without incident, and is dying to pull over into a shopping center, to decompress and figure out what the hell just happened.

DON'T STOP. YOU'RE COVERED IN HIS BLOOD. YOU GET PULLED OVER NOW, WE'RE FUCKED.

Anika keeps driving until she's finally home.

She lives on the third floor and has to take either the stairs or an elevator to reach her apartment. She might run into her neighbors, covered in blood.

She looks into the rearview. Only a bit of blood on her face.

She fumbles in her glove compartment, finds some wet napkins she took from the restaurant, and cleans up as best she can before shoving the bloody wipes into her purse.

But her clothes are still covered in Frankie's blood.

USE THE BLANKET. PEOPLE MIGHT THINK YOU'RE AVOIDING THE RAIN.

Better than nothing.

She gets out of the car, grabs her purse with the gun, pills, and enough evidence to screw her hard. She wraps the blanket around her.

The rain picks up, coming down even harder. Good, she can't afford to run into anyone on her way to the elevator.

She gets in, cold and shaking, desperate to go home, strip and stand beneath a long hot shower. She presses the button for the fourth floor. Looks down at the blanket while waiting for the door to close, barely covering her bloody clothes.

She can still smell it, moist and metallic.

If anyone gets close enough to her, they'll smell it too.

Someone comes running as the door is grinding closed. Shoves a hand in to stop the elevator from cutting her off.

Anika steps back as a young black girl from the floor below gets in. She's eleven, maybe twelve, wearing a purple raincoat and carrying two plastic bags of groceries.

She only knows the girl in passing. Doesn't know her name.

She looks at Anika suspiciously as the doors close and the elevator lurches up. "You okay?"

Her heart's beating so loud the girl can probably hear it. She's suddenly convinced that blood is dripping onto the floor, but she doesn't dare look down and draw her attention. The girl might scream and run to her parents. They'll call the police and everything will be over.

She's still staring.

Anika finally shakes her head. "No. Sick as a dog."

She coughs into her blanket.

The girl doesn't back away or flinch. She just stares.

DIDN'T YOUR MAMA TEACH YOU THAT STARING IS IMPOLITE?

The elevator dings at the third floor.

It slides open behind the girl. But she's staring at Anika instead of leaving.

SHE KNOWS SOMETHING'S WRONG! SHE KNOWS!

The girl backs out of the elevator, never breaking eye contact.

"Hope you feel better, miss," she says as the door is closing.

It finally shuts and Anika sighs in relief.

SCALDING WATER NEVER FELT BETTER.

Anika is on her shower floor. Pink water circles the drain. Hot water pounds on her shoulders. She only wishes she could make the water hotter, make it come down harder, as if it could wash the day away.

Only now can she finally process what happened.

She killed a man in self-defense, after her rape.

She's sore between her legs, bleeding there too. Bruises on her hips where Frankie must've grabbed her.

A fuzzy flashback, a snippet of a memory from when she was younger. This has happened before. Not exactly *this*, but something close.

Why can't I remember what happened?

How far did he go?

A horrifying thought — what if she's pregnant?

Anika wonders if she should go to the cops and report the assault.

THEY WILL ARREST YOU FOR HIS MURDER.

It was self-defense!

THEY WON'T CARE. WE CANNOT GO TO JAIL. DO YOU UNDERSTAND ME, ANIKA?

She can't think now. It's all too much.

Her head is pounding, a large egg on the back where Frankie might have hit her, or maybe she fell and smacked into something. Her adrenaline fades, and the pain is like a piano on her toes. Her mind spirals around a possible pregnancy.

What will she do? She can't possibly keep it.

God no.

WE'LL GET A MORNING-AFTER PILL TOMORROW. DON'T WORRY ABOUT IT.

IT'S OVER NOW.

But is it? Anika can't get the thoughts of Frankie out of her head, him drugging her, violating her. Thoughts swell with memories. It's a fire in her mind.

She remembers her therapist.

Her heart is raging. She can feel it throughout her entire body, thrumming.

What was his name?

How he sat beside her. She felt safe — until she didn't.

He touched her.

Heartbeat faster, anxiety tightening across her chest, squeezing the breath from her lungs like life from a gasping throat.

Has this happened before?

Why can't I remember?

Why can't I fucking remember?

The confusing knot of memories is swelling with the pain, spreading through Anika like a cancerous rot, swirling into a vortex that might tear her to pieces if deprived of its venting.

Heart racing, too fast now.

She can't breathe.

Her chest feels like an impossible weight is crushing her.

She wants to take all of this shit inside her and vent it in an explosion. The kind that demolishes a city block, incinerating her and the world around her.

Everything gone.

She screams.

Loud, not caring who hears, or might call the cops.

Anika screams until she's empty.

Her heartbeat finally slows.

The tightness in her chest disappears.

Fear subsides to a dull and throbbing ache.

Until she feels nothing.

But Anika has a way to fix that.

She gets out of the shower and finds her pills.

TWENTY-ONE

Delaney

I'm driving home in the rain, longing to unwind with a drink or five as I try and unpack what happened today.

Neither Father nor Brother Clarence came back.

I've spent the last couple of hours trying to make sense of it all. First, where did Brother Clarence go? And why did he come and leave like that?

His timing, just as Father seemed like he was going to tell me something about my mother, couldn't have been worse. And the more I think about it, the less a coincidence I think it is.

Brother Clarence is the only other person in this world who might know where Mother is, or was, if she's no longer alive. He was Father's right-hand man. He handled every problem. Including dealing with some of the crooked people trying to shake my father down, or helping him sway local politicians. A smooth-talking man, with soft speech that demanded respect.

Brother Clarence dealt with the police and the media after Mother's disappearance, while Father was holed up in his room for months, depressed. He carried the church in Father's absence, until he eventually returned.

Finally, with no leads, the police stopped looking.

But I never did.

Yet, despite my psychic gifts, and access to a vast network of information, I've yet to find any trace of what happened. It's like one day my mother just stopped existing.

For a long time, I thought she'd left us. I hated her for not taking me, for leaving me with Father as he exploited me for his growing religious empire.

After a while I wondered if Father had killed her. I hate thinking that. Despite all he's done to me, I don't hate him. Or think him capable of murder. Still, I've considered it more than once.

And if he did kill her, Brother Clarence would know where the body was buried. Maybe he shoveled the dirt on her grave. I think I would've gotten a flash of memory from one of them. The bigger the secret, the more it needs to leak out from their souls.

In the years that followed Mother's disappearance, I never got anything from either of them.

Brother Clarence fled town after Father got busted. I reached out a few times to see if maybe he remembered anything, but he never returned my calls. We lost touch, and I eventually forgot about him.

Until this morning.

And now I can't stop thinking about him.

The man looks exactly the same.

And Father said he'd come to him in a dream. Maybe Brother Clarence has a gift, like me.

I haven't run into anyone like myself, with any other ability, psychic or otherwise. But clearly *something* is up with Brother Clarence. Now that I think about it, I've always sensed something different about him, same as I've always sensed something different about my neighbor. But while Seb's energy is powerful yet kind, there is something dark about Brother Clarence. I've always figured I was picking up on his shady involvement in my father's criminal enterprise, rather than any latent psychic abilities.

So, what makes him special? And, more importantly, why is he back in our lives?

The timing with Anika can't be a coincidence.

I GET HOME, draw a hot bath, and find Pumpkin sleeping on my bed. I pet him behind the ears and ask him how his day is going.

He looks at me as though annoyed that I woke him from his nap, as if he doesn't sleep twenty out of twenty-four hours per day.

"Nice to see you, too. Grumpy bastard."

I leave him be, grab a couple of cold beers from the fridge, bring them to the tub, and get in.

I close my eyes and lean back, surprised by my exhaustion.

I wake, startled. My phone ringing on the toilet seat next to the tub.

Gerard.

I let it go to voicemail. As I wait to listen to the message, I realize two things: my bathwater is cold, and the clock on my phone reads 9:17 p.m.

My beer bottle is floating in the tub.

I look at the other one on the ledge, but now it's warm.

I listen to Gerard's message.

"Hey, I'm downstairs. Can I come up? Del? I know you're home. Your car is here."

Shit. Why is he here?

I get out of the tub, dry off, throw on some sweats and a long-sleeved tee. I open the front door and step onto the walkway to find Gerard in front of Seb and Ned's place, hanging out with the two of them, chatting.

Brandy comes up to me, tail wagging before dropping onto the ground and displaying her belly for scratches.

I bend to oblige her, looking up at Gerard, annoyed. I'm letting him know that his showing up like this is bullshit, and that we're gonna have a talk when we get inside.

Ned asks how I'm doing.

We make small talk as Gerard shifts from foot to foot. Seb and I exchange a glance. He probably knows I'm agitated. Takes the cue and yawns. "Okay, you two, we'll see you later."

He nudges a surprised Ned toward their door, then calls Brandy and they head inside, leaving us alone on the walkway.

Gerard looks at me nervously. "I'm sorry, it just seemed like you were down earlier. I wanted to make sure you were okay."

"I'm fine. Just some bullshit with my father that I really don't wanna talk about."

"You know I'm here if you do want to talk, right?"

"That's sweet," I say, still annoyed, with him and myself.

Why do I get so worked up when Gerard is being the kind of attentive guy most girls want? I think back to him saying how much I'm like a guy — why am I so put off by his actions when I genuinely care about him?

If I really think about it, he's not *that* clingy. We go for days without talking and he hardly ever does shit like this. I guess I'm still irritated by his trying to sleep over. Still see it as a sign of disrespecting my boundaries. Even if it was unintentional, he's referenced my never letting him stay over enough times to question whether or not it was an accident.

Why don't you just tell him why? It's not like he doesn't know about your psychic shit.

I can't tell him about that. *I can't tell anybody about that.*

It would live in the back of his mind forever.

He's staring. I'm sure he wants me to invite him in. He drove all the way over here, not that I asked him to. I don't want anyone in my space, not with all this shit in my head.

I approach him with the smile he likes. Rest my hands on his shoulders and meet his eyes so he knows I'm not upset. That I still have feelings for him.

"Listen, hon. I'm exhausted. I fell asleep in the tub, which is why I look like shit. Can we talk tomorrow? We can go for a romantic dinner at Oakwood's Stonehouse, come back here and fuck like rabbits?"

He laughs.

One time he was fumbling with words, talking about the first time we had sex. He was going to say *made love*, but the phrase seemed to trip him up because of how much I avoid it. He searched for some other term that didn't sound so crass, and I suggested fucking like rabbits.

"You sure you're okay tonight?" Times he's sweet like this I just wanna protect him from the world. He's too nice for me, really.

"Yes, I'm good. I swear."

I kiss him softly on the mouth, just long enough to arouse him, to let him know we're good.

He smiles.

"I'll see you tomorrow," I promise.

"Tomorrow. And we'll fuck like rabbits."

"Yes," I say, with a teasing bite on his lip.

I head inside, grab a cold one from the fridge, and sit

on my couch until I either make sense of everything happening with Father, Brother Clarence, and Anika, or fall asleep.

I'm fine with either.

~

SLEEP WON.

I wake in the morning to a call from Dusty.

"I got somethin' for ya."

"What's that?"

"That girlfriend of the missing man, Anika. He's not the first guy to disappear around her."

"What do you mean?"

"I thought her name sounded familiar. Anika's not that common a name, so I stopped by the station and looked through some old files."

"They let you do that?"

He laughs like the question is ridiculous. "Anyway, like ten years ago or so, this therapist goes missing. Just poof, gone. His wife called us to report it. She gave us a list of his clients and one of them was this skittish thirteen-year-old named Anika. I interviewed the girl and didn't think much of it then. Eventually, without a body, a suspect, or a crime scene, the case went icy. But I looked her up and she's very much the same Anika that was dating your guy, Jay. And that, my friend, is a bit too odd for an old-fashioned coincidence."

TWENTY-TWO

Anika

Anika wakes up feeling like she's been run over by a truck.

Her head is spinning, body aching everywhere, and she can barely sit up. She glances at the clock. It's ten past nine in the morning. She's supposed to be at work by three.

She has one more day to pay Rufus and so far she has nothing.

She picks up her phone and calls Chelsea.

Her sister answers on the third ring. "Hey, sis."

"Can we meet for breakfast?" Anika asks.

"I already ate, but yeah, we can meet. You okay?"

"Not really." Her voice cracks. The pain of everything is threatening to surface, so she does what she's always done and pushes it down.

"What's wrong?" Chelsea asks.

"I'll tell you in person."

They agree to meet at a bagel shop a few miles from Chelsea. Anika hangs up and shuffles to the bathroom, every movement introducing new pain into her body. She's desperate for another pill.

But Chelsea will know she's using again and get mad.

Anika can't take that kind of rejection. She needs help. And, loath as she is to ask for it, she must.

She showers, gets dressed, and slips two pills into her pocket — just in case.

The morning is cold and gray, the streets slick with rain as she drives to the bagel shop, struggling with the pain and a head full of cotton. A pill would cure her, but still she resists.

Anika thinks about the bottles she unloaded into her nightstand. Several of them, mostly painkillers, one a drug she didn't recognize and the bottle had no label. She probably has more than five hundred of them, maybe more. Enough to last her a while.

She can't go down that path. She made it more than three months before her relapse. But given her situation and stressors, who wouldn't succumb to pills? Still, she doesn't need to let history repeat itself. She can get clean again. Flush the pills and get back on the road to sobriety.

Once she's ready.

Anika arrives at the bagel shop before Chelsea, so she gets a table in the back and orders a coffee. She would get one for her sister, but doesn't want to presume she still drinks the same thing she did when they met more regularly.

The bagel shop is long and narrow like a shotgun shack, tightly cramped, filled mostly with older patrons all talking like regulars. Friendly, but the quarters are too close, making Anika claustrophobic.

The caffeine barely dents her headache.

She's rehearsing what she'll say. Looks up as the door opens and the tiny bell clangs against the glass. A pair of police officers enter, two men, one black and one Hispanic, both in their late thirties or early forties.

The black guy says, "Hey, Lou," to the fat old Italian man behind the counter.

"Hey, guys, how's it goin'?" Lou's voice is loud but friendly.

They're making small talk. Lou asks if they want their regulars. They both do.

The Hispanic cop glances back toward Anika.

Familiar panic claws at her chest.

They know. They know what I did and they're here to get me.

She looks down at the coffee, adds sugar to distract herself. To make it look like she couldn't care less about the cops, terrified as she is of their gazes.

RELAX. NOBODY EVEN KNOWS HE'S GONE YET.

How do you know that? Maybe he has a roommate or a girlfriend or someone who noticed the blood everywhere.

She looks back up.

Now they're both looking at her.

No!

She quickly looks down.

OH MY GOD, DON'T BE SO OBVIOUS! YOU MAY AS WELL SCREAM, "NOT GUILTY!"

She looks back up. The cops are talking to Lou, but the Hispanic one keeps looking back toward her.

Her pulse is as tight as her chest.

She looks down, then back up to see him suddenly walking toward her.

No, no, no, no!

She looks down at her cup, stirring the sugar, metal spoon clanking against the mug.

No, no, no, no!

She sees him in her peripheral vision, still coming toward her, but she can't look back up. There's no way to hide the guilt in her eyes.

RELAX!

He's a few feet from her table and still approaching.

Here we go. He's going to arrest me. They found Frankie's body.

I took a shower, so I can't even prove he raped me.

She imagines the cuffs. Booked and fingerprinted. Sees the cops talking to Chelsea, her name and photo in the news, people judging her guilty, no one believing the truth.

She holds her breath, bracing for her world to implode as the cop draws nearer, now inches away.

She closes her eyes, tears welling up, her throat so tight she's afraid she'll choke.

And then he passes.

What?

Her body is a current, waiting to explode.

She turns and sees the men's restroom door swinging shut.

She exhales, though the panic still has its fingers at her throat.

What if he comes back?

YOU'VE GOT PILLS IN YOUR POCKET. YOU'RE SCREWED.

She reaches into her pocket, grabs the pills and swallows them with a mouthful of hot coffee. Winces through the burn. Holds the mug with both hands, fingers tight as she waits for the cop to come out of the bathroom.

She hears the door swing open.

Hears his footsteps approaching.

She wants to turn back, but doesn't dare.

She waits.

He eventually passes, joins his partner at the counter. They talk with Lou before he hands them a big paper bag.

"Thanks, Lou," they both say before turning to leave.

The Hispanic cop looks back one last time at Anika.

Her eyes fall to the floor, praying he was checking her out and not seeing her guilt.

She takes another sip of coffee.

The server, a thin red-headed older woman named Kathy, asks if she's ready to order.

"I'll wait. She'll be here soon," Anika says.

But ten minutes later, she regrets not having food in her stomach. The pills are kicking in big time, just as Chelsea arrives.

She stands to greet her sister with a hug, then sits as Kathy comes over.

Chelsea orders a coffee, no food. Anika orders French toast and bacon. Another coffee to try and offset the drowsy lull of the pills before Chelsea notices.

"What's wrong?" Chelsea asks once their server is gone.

Though Anika had been rehearsing, her mind is suddenly foggy. Words are rubber. She laughs at the absurdity. She's finally found the courage to ask her sister for help, but she's too damned high to assemble the words.

"You okay?" Then her eyes widen. "Oh my God. You're using again, aren't you?"

Anika looks around, certain that someone must've heard. She's loud, but no one is paying attention. "It's not like that."

"You promised me. You *promised*," Chelsea says, eyes tearing up.

"Why are you so upset? You haven't even let me talk."

"Because you promised me."

"Well, this isn't about you." Anger douses her high.

Chelsea grabs a twenty from her purse, drops it on the table and stands. "I can't do this again."

"Do *what?*"

"*This!*" Chelsea yells, now drawing the diner's attention. "I can't sit here and watch you throw your life away."

She rushes out in tears.

Anika follows her out to the parking lot.

Chelsea is getting into her SUV.

Anika catches up and grabs her by the arm. "Please, don't go."

Chelsea spins, tears streaming down her face. "What? Do you want to tell me it was a mistake, that you won't do it again?"

"No. I need a favor."

"What?" Chelsea laughs. "A favor? Your dealer cut you off? Junkie boyfriend needs cash again?"

Again?

Chelsea's eyes narrow on her. "Oh, yeah, Stuart told me he gave you money six months ago."

Shit.

"Why didn't you ask me?"

"Because of this! I didn't want you judging me."

"So you went and asked my husband, whom you don't even know, for money to pay off your junkie boyfriend's drug debt?"

Chelsea reaches into her purse, grabs her wallet, and starts pulling bills out and throwing them at Anika. "How much does he need this time? Huh? Here, take it all!"

She pushes past Anika, gets in her vehicle, and slams the door, leaving Anika staring after her in shock as she tears out of the parking lot.

Her world has slipped away, and all the pills in her nightstand are no better than a few dirty sponges to soak up an oil spill.

TWENTY-THREE

Anika

Anika sits in the parking lot of the jewelry shop staring at the necklace sitting in her palm.

She realizes just how few memories are left of her mother. It feels as if someone has taken an eraser to her past, slowly removing one childhood recollection after another.

Her therapist from a couple of years ago said Post Traumatic Stress Disorder can do that. The mind can overwrite memories that are too difficult to remember.

She wishes she could keep the happy ones. There are so few.

Anika flashes back to her childhood. Mommy wearing the necklace with her best Sunday dress. Coming home and taking a nap with her on the couch.

Mommy had fallen asleep before her, and Anika was looking at the necklace resting on her bosom. She'd never dared to touch it, but now that she was asleep, Anika traced a finger along the gleaming pendant, admiring its sparkly beauty.

She had one of her first adult, scary realizations while

watching her sleeping. She thought Mommy had died. Only for a moment, but that was enough. Anika stared for what felt like the longest seconds of her life until she finally started breathing again. Even though she wasn't dead, that was the first time Anika realized that someday she would be.

And a horror show played in her core.

It was all she could think about most nights before sleeping. Nightmares on repeat, her mother dying in every one of them. Mommy gave her comfort when she woke up, always asking Anika what she had dreamed about.

But she could never tell her. Saying it seemed like her death might become a reality.

So she made up things about monsters or being lost. But her biggest fear was that someday she would lose her mommy. And, now, as Anika sits in her car outside the jewelry shop, she realizes again how much she still misses her. Part of her feels sure that selling the necklace means saying farewell to her memories.

But Anika is out of options. Without the cash, she's dead.

She stares at the shop's front door and finally works up enough courage to get out of her car and cross the parking lot in spite of her trembling hands.

The shop is small, run by a short balding old man in a tight powder-blue polo over a swollen gut. He's seated on a stool behind a jewelry case up front, tinkering with a watch.

He sets it on a white cloth and looks up from behind his Coke-bottle lenses.

"Welcome to Saul's Jewelry," he says, not remembering her from the previous visit when she'd come and had the necklace appraised — at Jay's insistence.

"Hi," she says, offering her widest smile. "I came in last year with a necklace you offered to buy."

"Oh?" He looks at her inquisitively. "And you've come to sell it?"

Reluctantly she says, "Yes."

"Let's see."

She reaches into her coat, withdraws the necklace, and sets it into his large hands.

He retrieves a jeweler's loupe from his pants pocket and inspects the necklace, making interesting *hmmm* and *huh* sounds as he examines it for a while.

The longer he holds it, the more Anika longs to snatch it back. The thought of some stranger holding Mommy's necklace feels like a betrayal.

Anika wonders what she would think of her. How disappointed Mommy would probably be with how her daughter turned out.

He looks up at Anika. "I'll give you sixty-five hundred."

"What? You told me it was worth fifteen grand!"

"That's retail, ma'am, what a shop would sell it for. That's not the price *I'd* pay."

"That's not enough." Her voice is cracking. She doesn't want to cry, but isn't above it if she thinks it will move him. But all the tears in the world aren't getting this guy to pay retail.

She feels stupid, and defeated.

Her last ray of hope to pay Rufus is gone.

She's about to grab the necklace and leave, but that inner voice stops her.

TAKE IT. OFFER IT TO RUFUS. TELL HIM THAT'S THE BEST YOU CAN DO.

IT'S BETTER THAN THE NOTHING HE HAS NOW, RIGHT?

HE'LL HAVE TO TAKE IT.

But … it's Mommy's necklace. It's worth more than what he's paying.

IT'S AS GOOD AS WE'RE GONNA GET. TAKE IT. WE'LL FIGURE SOMETHING OUT.

Anika swallows her lump. "Okay."

"What was that?" the man asks.

"It's yours."

~

ANIKA IS GOING through the motions at work, registering little, still numb from the pain and its supposed killers.

She's standing behind the register covering for Jolene, who is out on a smoke break. Normally, Anika would be annoyed about her missing tables, but it's slow and she doesn't care if she gets another one all day. She's wrapping utensils in cloth napkins, a chore she normally hates, but is finding rare comfort in the old familiarity.

Anika seats a party of twelve that should've been hers, so she's easily lost a large tip, but she doesn't care. She even seats them with Candi.

Whatever.

Nothing matters now.

She's lost her sister, and the last thing she had of her mother.

And she might lose her life if Rufus refuses the cash.

WE COULD TAKE THE MONEY AND RUN.

She considers it, but Rufus might make good on his threat to kill Chelsea and her family.

SO WHAT. Chelsea HATES US NOW.

No, she doesn't. She's just disappointed. Even if she hates me, that doesn't mean she should die.

Besides, Chelsea's right. I screwed things up. I chose to keep dating Jay even after I knew what he did for a living. Even after he started being verbally, then physically, abusive.

I chose to take the pills.

I can't run and let Chelsea, or, God forbid, her daughter, pay for my sins.

This is my mess to clean up.

Anika is lost in thought and the mindless wrapping of utensils when she spots her audience. Rufus, smiling.

No longer numb, she's been snapped into the moment, her heart now racing.

"I believe you have something for me."

"I've got one more day." She looks around to make sure none of her coworkers are watching or within earshot.

She has privacy, for now.

"And, how's it going?"

"I'm still getting the money together."

He points at his wrist, though there's no watch. "Tick-tock, motherfucker."

He turns to leave.

"Wait," she says.

He turns back, eyebrow cocked. *"Yessss?"*

"I sold the only thing I have of value, a necklace my mom left me. It's worth fifteen grand, but the guy at the jewelry shop only gave me sixty-five hundred. I can give you that, but … I don't have another way to come up with the rest, at least not as quickly as you need."

"How long's it gonna take?"

"I … I don't know. I've been trying to get the money, but … it's difficult. It's not like I have any rich friends dying to give me money."

"Ask your sister."

"I did. She doesn't have it."

"A nice house like that and she don't have it?"

"They're mortgaged up to their necks. They owe the

IRS a ton of back taxes and are barely hanging on," Anika lies, hoping he believes her.

"You got this sixty-five hundred on you?"

"Yes." She's hopeful that he might accept what she has and move on. "Hold on a minute."

Anika races to the back room, opens her locker, and digs the cash from her purse. She looks at the pistol, wondering if she should take it with her, just in case Rufus tries something.

OR YOU CAN END IT RIGHT NOW AND KILL THE BASTARD!

Except she could never just kill someone in cold blood.

She leaves the pistol, slips the cash into her apron pocket, and heads up front. She's about to hand Rufus the envelope when a family with a little blonde girl of about seven enters the restaurant.

The dad is telling her that he's meeting some people, and asking if he can be seated.

The little girl stares at Rufus. He smiles at her. Friendly rather than creepy, so out of place on a face full of ink.

Maybe he isn't heartless. Maybe he'll let me slide with sixty-five hundred.

She seats the family, then returns to Rufus and hands him the envelope.

He opens it in plain sight without any regard for who might see him. He looks at the bills then closes the envelope and slides it into the front right pocket of his jeans.

"This is good. I'll be back tomorrow for the rest."

He turns and leaves.

"Wait!"

Rufus ignores her.

Anika races after him, out into the parking and pouring rain. "Wait! That's all I have."

He keeps walking.

She runs toward him, then grabs his arm to pull him around and force him to listen.

He turns, his eyes full of rage as he grabs her hard by the throat. He slams her against a van, choking her as he leans in, his hot alcoholic breath in her face. "Do *not* fucking touch me."

A woman's voice comes from behind them. "Get your hands off of her!"

Both Anika and Rufus turn to see who's talking.

That nosy woman from the other day, and she has a gun aimed right at Rufus.

TWENTY-FOUR

Delaney

"I said get your fucking hands off of her!" I'm looking down the barrel of my pistol at the scumbag.

He slowly turns, letting go of Anika as he smiles and narrows his gaze at me. "This ain't your business."

"I beg to differ. What's going on here?"

I recognize the asshole from my research — Rufus T. Is he looking for Jay, shaking Anika down for whatever her boyfriend took, or something else?

Anika stares at me, too terrified for words.

I repeat my question to Rufus, gun still aimed squarely at his chest, though he doesn't seem especially frightened. I doubt this is the first time he's had a gun on him.

"Just catching up with an old friend." He backs away from both of us, then turns his back and continues to his red Impala.

I holster my gun and turn to Anika.

She's staring at me, eyes rimmed with tears. "So, you are a cop?"

"No."

"Then what are you doing here?"

"Jay's parents hired me to find him."

From scared to pissed: "Why didn't you just say that instead of coming into my restaurant and lying to me?"

"I didn't lie."

"You were being sneaky, talking about … never mind." She walks away, toward her car.

"Wait!"

Anika turns. "What?"

"What was all that about?"

"Nothing."

"Didn't look like nothing. You wanna tell me so I can help, or would you rather let him come back and finish whatever that was?"

She wipes at her eyes. "He wants money."

"For?"

"He says Jay stole a bunch of his drugs. Since I don't know where he is, I have to pay him."

"How much?"

"Fifteen grand. I sold something to get sixty-five hundred."

"And you gave it to him?"

"What else was I gonna do? He said if I went to the cops or took off, he'd hurt my sister."

"The cops could've helped you." Or maybe not. If Rufus is as bad as Dusty said, there's nothing the police could do. Guys like that don't care about the cops' minimal efforts to protect her — assuming they'd do anything.

"He has people watching me."

"So, you gave him the sixty-five and now he wants the rest?"

"Yes."

"By when?"

"Tomorrow."

"Fuck."

"Yeah." A long, exhausted sigh. "I don't know what to do. That necklace was all I had."

"And you don't know where Jay is?"

"No," she says, sharply.

The rain comes harder.

"Can we talk? I'm sure we can come up with something to resolve this."

She looks at me for a long moment. She has no reason to trust me, but few other options.

Thunder makes her jump. And in that moment, I sense something under the surface. Something that gives me a weird sense of déjà vu. For a split second it feels like I'm standing with someone other than Anika.

But that sensation is gone as fast as it came.

She nods. "Okay, anywhere but here."

"I've got a place."

WE CLIMB INTO A QUIET, private booth in the back of Dusty's pub, far away from anyone wanting to eavesdrop.

The booth is dark. Tall walls so no one can see us unless they walk over. I've had many private conversations here. Dusty is good about keeping people from sitting too close.

He comes over and takes our order with a wink before returning to the bar.

Anika doesn't drink alcohol, so she orders a Coke, which lessens the odds of me loosening her tongue. I order a whiskey to calm my nerves. After pulling my gun on Rufus, I need to unwind.

Dusty brings our drinks and leaves the bottle of Jack with a grin. "Figured I'd save myself the walk."

"You know me too well, Dusty."

"If there's anything you ladies need, just holler."

"He looks familiar," Anika says after he leaves.

She seems to genuinely not remember him, which makes sense. How many people remember someone from the other side of a conversation when they were thirteen?

"He has one of those faces." I down the whiskey and pour myself another.

Anika is staring at the table, fingers caressing the cold beads of water on her Coke.

"What happened with Jay?"

She answers, not looking up to meet my eyes. "What do you mean?"

"Did he say anything before he left? Do you know what he did with Rufus's stash?"

"I don't know anything. He didn't say anything."

"So, he just vanished without any sign of something wrong? What's the last thing he said? Was he acting weird? Nervous? Scared?"

"It's all kind of fuzzy. I can't remember the last time I saw him. I think it was a couple days before he disappeared. We'd gone to dinner and I had a migraine so I went home early. But I'm honestly not sure if that was the last time. Sometimes he'd be off doing his own thing for a few days at a time, then I'd get a call and he'd wanna hang."

"Sounds casual. Were you two not especially close?"

"Define *close*." Anika finally meets my eyes. I see a familiar pain, the same one haunting so many abused women and children.

"Were you exclusive? Did he have other women on the side? Did you? Men, I mean … or women, if that's your thing?"

"I didn't have anyone else. And I don't think he did.

Work kept him busy. He knew I didn't like when he was all coked up, so he avoided me when he was."

"That his drug of choice?"

"Jay did everything."

"And you didn't like it?"

"No."

"Anti-drug?"

She flinches, just a bit but it's there. "Seems self-destructive, don't you think?"

I pour myself a third whiskey. I'm pouring small amounts, but acting more intoxicated than I am. Sometimes it helps people loosen up if they think I'm tipsy. Anika might let something slip if she thinks I'm not paying close attention.

I raise my glass. "Here's to a little self-destruction."

She smiles, raises her Coke to clink against my whiskey, and finally takes a drink.

"What's he like?" I ask, intentionally not using past tense.

"Jay?"

"Yeah."

"He was sweet sometimes. An asshole others."

Was. Past tense.

Is that because she knows he's dead or figures he's gone?

"What else? How'd you two meet?"

She tells me how they met, a year or so ago, at her restaurant. He came in a lot, tipping her like crazy but never outright flirting. She eventually asked him out. He seemed shy at first, and was. Except when he was partying, then Anika never knew what she'd get. Sometimes it was exciting, an adrenaline rush to be with him, driving fast, doing crazy shit. Other times, he got mean. That's when Anika avoided him.

"Did he ever hit you?"

She pauses, then says no.

I don't believe her.

We talk more about Jay, me listening, letting her navigate the conversation as I pretend to slur my words a bit.

I bring the conversation back to the last time she saw him, but Anika doesn't remember much about that last time, or she's lying. I'm frustrated not knowing which.

"What do *you* think happened to him?" I take another drink of Jack.

"I don't know. A lot of times we used to lie in bed at night and that's when I felt he was most real, instead of putting on an act. He'd talk about just wanting to leave it all behind — the life, his family. He said he'd take me to Canada and we could start over."

"So you think he did that alone?"

"I don't know why he wouldn't have taken me if he did."

Anika seems genuinely hurt. Despite my first impressions, I'm thinking maybe she doesn't know what happened to him.

"Was he maybe cheating on you? Ever see strange texts or anything he didn't want to explain? Maybe he left with someone else?"

She looks down, closing her eyes, then back up at me. Something has changed within her. I can't tell what. It's not her expression or anything I can pinpoint, but that feeling is back from before, like I'm having a conversation with someone else.

"Now that you mention it, he hid his phone a lot. He'd say the power was low or something whenever I wanted to use it. Maybe he was cheating on me. And left with someone else."

I see the faintest hint of a smile. Barely there, only for a nanosecond, creeping at the corners of her mouth, but I know what I saw.

She's playing me.

But then I remember Father's warning.

That girl has the devil in her.

It knows what you are.

Is she possessed? Is that the thing I'm sensing inside her?

But demons aren't real. For all Father's talk, and my healing people from sickness by driving them out, I've never once seen a demon.

Have I?

A glimpse of a memory or a dream — me, as a child with a shriveled old man in a wheelchair. It's gone before I can flesh it out or follow the image to its conclusion.

What if Father's not crazy?

I meet Anika's eyes and can't shake the feeling that there's something hiding inside this girl, far older and wiser than I am, staring back at me.

"So, what can I do about Rufus?"

I have to hide my sudden annoyance with being lied to. Keep playing like I don't know if I'll ever get the truth. I can't let the something inside her know I'm onto it.

"I'll talk to Rufus."

"And say what?"

"Tell him that the store's closed. If he makes a move on you or your sister, he's fucked."

"How?"

"I've got an idea." But I don't.

"You sure he won't come after my sister?"

"Your sister will be safe. You both will be." Despite my promise, I'm already planning on tailing Anika to find out exactly what she knows — and what she's done.

TWENTY-FIVE

Delaney

I head to the nursing home after dropping Anika back off at the restaurant.

Father is taking a nap in his room. His nurse lets me in and closes the door.

I stand over Father looking down at the frail man I once loved so much, and feared even more. I wish I could feel something for him again. Wish our lives had taken different paths — one where Mother never left and Father didn't use my powers to exploit people out of their money. One where I didn't have trust issues. Where maybe I didn't have this damned curse and could sleep next to someone without seeing the things I see.

But what's the point of wishing for things that cannot be?

I shake Father awake.

He looks up, startled. "Delaney?"

Good, he's cogent — for now.

"We need to talk."

He sits up, concern knitting his brow as he grabs his

glasses from the nightstand and slips them on. "What's wrong?"

I pull up a chair next to his bed. "I need you to be honest with me."

His lips tighten and he looks like he's going to sigh, but I barrel on. "I think someone might be in danger and I'm not sure if I'm seeing what I think I'm seeing."

He leans forward, curious and concerned. "What is it?"

"Do you really believe there are demons inside people, making them sick? That make them do bad things? Or was that something you told the flock?"

"Are you really asking me that? After all you've seen?"

"I don't remember much of my childhood, so I don't know what I've seen. It's all a blur."

He swallows and nods. "I'm sorry about that."

"What do you mean?"

"We thought it would be better if you didn't remember it all."

"Remember what? Who thought it would be better?"

His eyes dart around like he's nervous, or maybe said too much. "Never mind."

"I deserve to know."

"Trust me, Delaney. You don't want to know. But I will answer you as best I can."

I sigh. That'll have to do for now. "Okay."

"Yes, demons are real. That's my word. Brother Clarence calls them something else." He looks up like he's trying to remember something. "Damn, I can't remember ... you can call them monsters. But they're not from Hell."

"What do you mean?"

"They're from somewhere else, something Brother Clarence called the In-Between."

"The In-Between? What does that even mean?"

He takes my right hand and raises it. "Hold it straight up."

I do.

He puts his hands on either side of mine. They're surprisingly warm. It occurs to me that I can't remember the last time my father touched me other than the times he'd hold my hand before introducing me to his parishioners.

"My left hand, let's call that Heaven."

I roll my eyes. He knows I don't believe in the place.

"Maybe it's not what the Bible says, but it is a place, whether you believe it or not."

"Fine. Go on."

"My other hand is Earth and all the other realms."

"Other realms?"

"And your hand … that's In-Between, a place between us and heaven. Sometimes things escape and infest our world. They make us sick or drive us to do terrible things."

"You going to say a demon, or monster, was inside you when you bilked those people out of their money, and slept with all those women?"

"Yes, in fact, it was."

I pull my hand away. "Can you for once even take responsibility for what you did instead of blaming it on fucking *demons?*"

"You know it's true, Delaney. You've seen them. You've pulled them out of people. That was your gift and you were great at it."

Tears well up in his eyes as he remembers some idealized version of me he once used like an ATM. But I'm not that little girl anymore. And I won't put up with this bullshit.

"It was a mistake coming here. Clearly, you have lost your mind."

He grabs my hand as I stand.

And suddenly, I'm back in my childhood.

I'M on stage with Father, Mother, and Brother Clarence.

They're bringing that man up. The mayor, twisted in pain.

His sunken eyes look up to meet mine. But he's not gazing my way like the others. He's looking a way I don't recognize but feel in my bones.

Father takes my hands and puts them on the mayor's.

In an instant, everyone is gone.

The church vanishes. There is only darkness. Me and the mayor in his wheelchair.

And someone else. Or something. It's inside the mayor, watching me with cold, dark eyes.

"Hello, child," says its sickening voice in my head. *"We meet at last."*

I remember my training. The sickness inside some people twists enough to invite demons inside.

But I don't have to be scared.

I'm a child of God.

And He's given me a gift.

"Out, demon!" I yell.

The thing inside the mayor laughs, his ancient face crumpling into a smile of mockery.

"I said out, demon!" I step forward, raising my hand.

It's burning bright, reflecting in the mayor's suddenly terrified eyes.

"Out, demon!"

He's no longer laughing, or leaving.

I'm going to force him out.

I move closer.

My mind is filled with scary images — my mother

being torn in half by a chainsaw-wielding masked man; my father holding a blade in one hand and a baby in the other; and my friend Charlotte in church being ripped to pieces by the congregation. First her clothes, then her flesh.

I know these are the demon's lies, but they feel real. They feel horrible, and I want to back away so I'm no longer forced to see them.

I feel my father's hands on my back, his voice in my ear. "Do not fear him, my child. You are stronger."

Father isn't here with me in this dark place, but back in the real world, where my body is going through these motions. I have to trust he won't let anything hurt me.

That Father will catch me if I fail.

I push against the images.

"They'll alllllll die," screams the mayor's monster. *"Everything you've ever loved will dieeeeeeeeee."*

"Liar!" I put my hand on his head.

More images assaulting me, things I'll never unsee, bleeding into my brain.

I'm crying, certain I'm going to crack like a porcelain plate dropped on the patio.

Father steadies me. "That's it, Delaney, he's on the ropes. Finish it."

I put both hands on the mayor's head.

He screams, so loud my skull might crack.

"You've got him!" Father shouts. "Do not let the demon sway you!"

Brother Clarence has a vial of holy water. He's splashing it on the mayor, saying, "Be gone, demon!"

He and Father are chanting in a strange language, repeating a complicated-sounding phrase as the mayor thrashes.

More horrifying images, and now nothing makes sense. I barely know who I am or what I'm doing.

But I've not forgotten my mission, what I must do.

"Out, demon!"

The images stop.

The mayor's face contorts into a scream, but there's no sound. Only a swirling darkness, smoke but thicker. Liquid, moving fast, a tornado on my body.

I maintain my grip on the mayor's head, my body buffeted by darkness as it holds the assault, now pouring into my nose and mouth, maybe even my ears.

It's choking me, but I maintain my grip.

Father won't allow me to fail.

The church windows, though I can't see them, burst as parts of the darkness race out in search of escape.

My vision blurs at the edges. I gasp but draw only the darkness.

Choking, trying to spit it out, I keep holding on.

Until it's finally left the mayor.

The darkness has gone, and I'm back in the church standing before the mayor who is gasping for air himself.

I feel dizzy.

I fall.

I PULL AWAY from Father's hand, glaring at him.

"What the hell was that?"

"You remember now?"

"I almost died."

"But you succeeded instead. That was the last monster you exorcised."

"What happened after that?"

Father stares at me for a long moment.

"What happened after that?" I repeat.

"It doesn't matter. The point is, demons are real. And I

am not the monster you believed me to be. The demon you got rid of that day went into me."

"Into you?"

"Yes." Father stares at me as if questioning my faith.

But I'm not sure what I believe anymore. "So, what do I do about Anika?"

For a moment, he stares at me. "What do you mean?"

"You said she has a demon, or monster, inside her. How do I get it out?"

"You don't."

"What?"

"Avoid her at all costs. It knows what you are and it *will* destroy you."

"I can't just ignore it."

"You can't save the world, Delaney. Stop trying. Enjoy what time you have left."

I won't win this argument, so I ask something else. "How did you know about her?"

"Brother Clarence told me. Warned me."

"Where is he now?"

Father points to his head. "Up here until I need him again."

"What?"

He looks like he might be on the verge of slipping back into confusion. I can't sit here and debate him or request details he's never going to give me. I have to ask him things relevant to Anika and this case.

"What else do you know about her? What did she do?"

"I don't know." He shakes his head. "All I know is that there's a demon inside her, and it's a danger to you."

"How can I help her get rid of it?"

He pounds a fist on the table, eyes narrowing on me sharply like they did when I was a child who upset him. I'm back in time and afraid of him.

"Stay away from her!"

"I *have* to help her. Let's say you're right and there *is* a monster or whatever. How do I get it out of her?"

"The only way is to kill her."

"I can't *kill her!*"

"You're right. Because if you do, the demon will need a new home."

"There must be *something* I can do."

"Maybe." Father stares off in thought, concocting some plan to rid Anika of her monster. I'm still not sure if I'm buying his shit, but I've seen enough to know I can't ignore what might seem impossible. There's a whole world of weird out there, maybe even an In-Between, and I've felt strange things right under my nose ever since I can remember.

"Maybe …" Father repeats before trailing off.

"Maybe what?"

"Maybe they have pudding tonight? Do you think they'll have pudding?"

Shit.

Father's gone again.

TWENTY-SIX

Delaney

I'm driving from the nursing home and thinking how best to handle the Anika situation. I need a conversation with someone closer to Rufus.

Skeezy.

I head to the small computer repair shop Keshawn told me about, in an aging shopping center on the south side.

I park on the cracked faded pavement and make a quick call to Marsha, leaving a message to update her that I'm still on the case and will call her with more details soon.

I get out of the car and enter the computer shop.

There's a fat bearded pale dude with dreads and a series of unfortunate-looking tattoo decisions lining his face sitting on a stool behind the counter. He' watching a video on his phone, laughing, not even looking as I enter.

Up close, the tattoos look even worse, like someone's awful attempt at Japanese characters and artistic flourishes. I wonder if the words have any meaning or if he pointed in a catalog and said, "Gimme that."

The shop is empty of customers, hardly a shock given

that the only stock on display are a few large-screen TVs on the wall, plus some tablets and phones that seem over-priced for older tech.

I approach the desk. He looks up and his sleepy eyes startle while checking me out.

"Hey," he says, standing and straightening his triple extra-large black tee over his faded red cargo pants. "How can I help you?"

He doesn't need a name tag. One of his face tattoos reads *Skeezy.* The only word sort of in English.

"My name is Del."

I offer my hand and he shakes it.

I get a few flashes of memory, quickest I've ever gotten anything on anyone.

I'm not sure if it's my knowing smile or if he somehow senses me probing him. Maybe he's leery, but he withdraws his hand, then looks at it as if expecting to see burn marks.

"I need some info, Stanley."

He steps back, eyeing me suspiciously. "And I need some, too, like who the hell you is comin' in here actin' like you know me. And the name is *Skeezy.*"

"I *is* a paying customer, and I understand you're the wise man 'round these parts." I fish a wad of bills from my jacket. "Friend said you could help me out. Was he wrong?"

He looks down at the cash, eyes fat with greed. "Depends. Whatcha lookin' to learn?"

"Big Jay, know of him?"

"Might be a hundo could jog my memory banks."

I slide two fifties across the counter. He pockets them, then proceeds to tell me shit I already know about Jay.

"That's all common knowledge." I give him a disap-pointed look. "I thought you'd know something worth something."

"Like what?"

"Where he went?"

"Dude's dead."

"And how do you know that?"

"Because you don't steal from Rufus T. and live to tell."

"Any chance a rival robbed him, set him up?"

"I suppose. Most people afraid to cross Rufus, though. 'Cept maybe the Asians. They ain't 'fraid of anyone."

"Who runs their crew?"

"Brother and sister, Li Xia and Wang Jie. But I don't think they'd have done it. They keep to themselves, know what I'm sayin'? Also, they rob more than dealers. Someone like Rufus don't merit attention unless he fucks with them, which he ain't dumb enough to do."

"So what do *you* think happened to the drugs, Stanley?"

"Hell if I know. Dude mighta used it all up. Dumbass."

"Okay, what can you tell me about Rufus?"

"Whatcha mean?"

"I want a weakness, or dirt I can use on him."

"What *kind of* weakness or dirt?"

"The kind that might get him to back off from a threat."

"You think I'm gonna rat out Rufus for some bitch I don't know?" He laughs.

"I'd hate for Wang Jie to find out about the shipment."

I'm not even sure what Wang Jie has to do with a shipment, but I got a flash when we shook, and his surprised expression is like a diorama of his anxiety.

"I don't know what you're talkin' 'bout."

"Okay, have fun explaining that to Wang Jie." I turn toward the exit.

"Wait."

"Yes?"

"Fine, I'll give you somethin' but it's gonna cost you a lot more than a hundo."

I could probably squeeze it out with a few more threats, but I'll let him save some face. Not my money, after all.

"How much?"

He looks me up and down. "Six."

"Six hundred dollars?"

"Yeah."

"Better be good shit."

"Oh, it is."

I slide six Benjamins across the counter.

He looks at me for a long moment. "He might straight up kill yo ass."

"I'll take my chances."

"Suit yourself. Rufus gots a place over on Magnolia and Temple, the pink apartment. He also gots some honies that barely be old enough to bleed."

He doesn't elaborate or need to, but he does give me a number for Rufus, so I don't have to deliver my threat in person. Which is great, because there's an excellent chance he's right. Rufus could call my bluff and kill me. Plus, I'll need time to put together my insurance policy.

"Thanks," I say.

"You paid that six hundo without flinching. I coulda charged you more."

"At least double," I tease with a wink. "Pleasure doing business with you, Stanley."

"It's *Skeezy*," he calls out as I leave.

TWENTY-SEVEN

Anika

Anika is lying in her warm bubble bath with soft music playing and candlelight flickering off the tiles as she finally relaxes, letting the pills carry her off in a wave of bliss.

Her mind is supposed to stop obsessing about her worries.

But she keeps thinking about Del, who promised to help her, and that Chelsea would be safe. Was she sincere, or saying whatever she needed to get her information? Jay's parents aren't good people.

He'd told her horror stories of growing up with his father. An egomaniacal, abusive monster. His mom let him wreak havoc on Jay's life.

Anika wonders if she can trust the woman. There's a lingering doubt in the back of her mind. She's been taken advantage of too many times by people offering to "help" her.

She gets flashes of memories in a staccato burst: her therapist when she was younger, sitting beside her; hiding in her bedroom, shaking as her dad screamed at her mom; then one that feels more recent — her scrubbing a floor with a wet rag, the overpowering reek of bleach in her nostrils.

She smells it even now, in the tub, as if the memory has transplanted past and present sensations.

She gets out of the tub, dries off, and slides into her pajamas. She longs to crawl under her covers and disappear into their warmth. Sleep until noon.

She leaves her bathroom and enters her bedroom. She thought she'd left a light on, but she's too tired to bother now. She plops into bed, pulls the covers over her, and closes her eyes.

A familiar sound wakes her — the shaking of a pill bottle, though she's not sure where it comes from.

Her light flicks on and she sees Rufus in the corner, leaning against the wall and holding one of the giant bottles she stole from Frankie.

She sits up and crawls back as close to her bed's headboard as she can get, trying to remember where her gun and phone are.

Both in her purse, in the kitchen.

Shit.

Rufus throws the bottle at her.

It bounces on the bed and lands right next her. She doesn't reach for it.

"Well, well, well, looks like someone got themselves quite the little stash."

"What are you doing in here?" Anika's voice is shaky.

Rufus stays in the corner, still casually leaning.

"Our conversation was interrupted. I hate to be interrupted."

"What do you want? I told you I don't have any more money."

"See, that's the thing. I think you're not trying hard enough. A debt is a debt and I don't let 'em slide."

"I don't owe you anything. That was Jay. And he took off!" Anika might be on the verge of tears, but her senses are also dulled.

"And yet here you are with a big stash of pills."

"Those aren't yours."

"But they're also not yours. They belong to an associate of mine. But, of course, you know that, don't you?"

Anika says nothing.

"What's that, two disappeared dealers, both with ties to you. And here you are, flush with drugs? Maybe I'm crazy, but this sure looks a little fucking suspicious, don't ya think?"

"I don't know what you're talking about."

"So you weren't at Frankie's house last night? Because homeboy's got footage suggesting otherwise."

No!

Her panic swells.

Rufus smiles. "Oh, yeah. I saw what he did to you. But, more importantly, I saw what *you* did to him."

"I don't know what you're talking about."

He snorts in disbelief. "I have a new proposal."

"What?"

"I have a little problem you can help me with. A problem you invited into my life with that damned PI."

"What about her?"

"She's been digging in some places where there shouldn't be shovels and I can't have that shit. You take care of her and we're cool."

"What do you mean, take care of her?"

"Do what you did to Frankie."

"I don't remember anything."

"No? Maybe this'll help." He smiles again and throws her a flash drive.

She catches it, barely.

"Don't worry, I've got copies. Anything happens to me, they get sent to someone who would be *very* interested in your abilities. Or … you could come work for me. I could use someone with your talents. Make lots of money, get all the pills you want." He throws her a cell phone. "Choice is yours. Call me when you've made up your mind."

Anika catches it.

"One last thing. You don't do it, your sister, her daughter, and her husband are all dead. I've got someone sitting on them now."

"You're lying."

He pulls out his phone and flips through until he finds what he wants to show her — a close-up shot of her sister, taken through a window.

"Remember that red light on you in the parking lot that day? My best guy. Never misses."

"If the PI is such a threat, why don't you have him take care of her?"

"Because, I looked into her. Boyfriend's a cop. I don't need that kinda heat. But you, well, *you've* been getting away with murder for some time now, haven't ya? Nobody thinks twice when you're involved. Such an innocent, ain't ya?"

A creepy wink and then he's gone.

Anika stares at the front door for a long time, shaking. The pills no longer able to numb her fear, it's now crashing in on her exponentially.

She rushes over and locks the door, even though Rufus had somehow broken in and could surely do it again.

She stares at the flash drive, wondering what the hell he's talking about. What could be on there?

One way to find out.

She gets her laptop, brings it to her bed, and plugs in the flash drive.

Maybe I shouldn't.

NO, IT'S TIME WE FINALLY MEET.

We?

A chill runs through her.

Anika's voice has never spoken as something other than another part of herself.

Now, it feels different. No longer like some smarter inner voice keeping her from doing stupid things with the occasional suggestion, or that voice picking her up when she's down. It sounds different, like something separate from her.

There's a single video file on the flash drive.

Her finger hovers over the mouse to click on it. She's shaking, afraid of what she's about to see. Some threshold with no return she's known about for some time, even if she had to believe her own lies to live with the secret.

Everything will change once she clicks.

I shouldn't. I should go to Del's and see what she suggests …

OR YOU CLICK AND SEE THE WORLD AS IT REALLY IS.

Anika's finger hovers forever, confusion burning her mind. These last few months have been a haze and only now is she seeing through the fog to the fire about to consume her. It took Jay. Next it will take Chelsea and Emery. Then finally her.

CLICK IT. WE CAN CHANGE ALL OF THIS.

She shouldn't. Some childlike part of her wants to maintain the blissful ignorance. It tells her to turn away before it's too late.

CLICK IT, ANIKA. CLICK IT AND LET US MOVE FORWARD TOGETHER.

It feels wrong.

Her hand is shaking and her throat is clenching up.

Her heart is racing as her chest feels like a steel band is tightening around it, threatening to squeeze until she pops.

Everything, other than the voice, is telling her to ignore it. Close the laptop and carry on.

CLICK IT!

CLICK IT!

CLICK IT!

CLICK IT!

CLICK IT!

CLICK IT!

CLICK IT!

Finally, Anika clicks.

TWENTY-EIGHT

Delaney

I'm sitting across from Gerard as dinner winds down, wishing I'd never agreed to this.

Dinner at Oakwood's Stonehouse was fantastic, and I have to admit I'm enjoying myself. The meal was perfect and the ambiance here always puts me in the mood. And as we both take bites from a chocolate bread pudding, I don't want the meal to end. But I'll have to cut the date short because I have to take care of the Rufus situation tonight.

I'm trying to figure out the best way to break the news to Gerard that we won't be "fucking like bunnies." He's going to be all bitchy about it.

"So, anyway," Gerard says after a sip of his wine, "this woman is going on and on about how she's worried that her dad is hurt or something. He hasn't answered the phone and she hasn't heard from him in three days. So we're thinking we're gonna find a body, right? We knock on the door, and nothing."

Another sip. "But we hear noise coming from inside. Sounds like someone struggling or maybe in pain. We knock again. Still nothing. So we breach, go in, guns drawn, and sweep the living room. Noises coming from a back bedroom. Someone crying. I can't tell if it's a man or woman, but I don't waste any time. I kick in the door, ready for anything, but …"

"What?"

"There's an eighty-three-year-old man lying on his bed, naked, with a VR set and headphones, watching hardcore bondage porn while pounding away at a Fleshlight."

"No!"

"Oh, yeah."

"So, what did you do? What did *he* do?"

"He didn't see us."

"What?"

"He was *really* going to town. Didn't hear us banging on his front door, didn't hear us kick it in. Didn't even hear us when we were watching him doing the jackhammer from his bedroom door."

"So what did you do?"

"We left."

"You *left?*"

"Yeah, what was I *supposed* to do, interrupt him? Probably give the old guy a heart attack."

"That whole story is awful."

"You prefer we found a body?"

"Well, no, but … God. So, what did you tell his daughter?"

"Said he was fine and left it at that. Wilson left a note on his nightstand: *Call your daughter.*

"No!"

Gerard is cracking me up, crying tears of laughter as he recalls Wilson leaving the card on the nightstand and imagining the look on the old man's face when he finally stopped jerking, saw his door kicked in, and read the note.

A moment of awkward silence as Gerard stares at me with this weird look in his eyes.

"What?" I ask.

"Nothing."

"No, you were thinking something; what is it?"

"It's just been a while since I've seen you this happy."

"What do you mean? I'm always a ray of fucking sunshine."

"You've been different lately … you know you can talk to me."

"I know." My wine is empty, so I grab my glass of ice water and drink it down, trying to conjure an escape from this conversation.

"Then why don't you?"

"Why don't I what?"

"Talk to me."

"We're talking now."

"Don't be so dense, Del. And don't think I don't know what you're doing."

"What?"

"You're trying to start a fight over something small so you can avoid a serious discussion."

I nod and say nothing.

"What's got you down? Is it your dad?"

"Nothing's got me down. Just the job, boring shit, you know?"

"Do you need money?"

"No," I say, standing.

"You leaving?"

"No, I'm going to the bathroom. Is that okay, or do you want to talk about *that*, too?"

Fuck! I'm such an asshole.

I want to turn back and apologize, but it's too soon. I need time or I might break down.

Too many emotions running through me. I need to collect myself so I don't start spewing everything at Gerard. There are things I want to tell him but can't. Not him or anybody else. No one would understand.

And that's before I learned about my past, pulling monsters out of people.

How the hell do I tell anybody that?

I don't have to pee. I need time to gather my shit. It'll also give me time to think up an excuse to end the date without him taking it as a dramatic response to our brewing argument.

I can come back and say I got a text from a client.

Sorry, hon. We'll fuck like bunnies tomorrow.

He'll get over it. Always does.

May as well pee while I'm in here. I'm sitting in my stall, checking my phone, killing a few minutes, seeing if Anika's texted. Nothing. I wonder what she's doing now. If she's home freaking out about Rufus, or …

I think about what Father said, his warning that there's a demon in her.

Could that be true?

It would've all seemed ridiculous before he triggered my memory.

Though maybe that wasn't real. I was brainwashed into his religion from an early age. There's lots of things he convinced me of that I now know aren't true. Could this be just one more thing?

Then how did I remember so many details?

I don't know. The brain is a remarkable puzzle-solving machine. It can manufacture shit so other crap makes sense. Maybe that whole thing with the mayor never happened.

In which case, Anika isn't possessed. She's a woman with an awful streak of luck.

Or maybe my psychic curse somehow worsened an existing illness or psychological problem. A delusion or madness that infected me.

Something about that makes sense. Maybe that's it. A scientific or psychological explanation, not some religious or supernatural bullshit. There's no such thing as monsters, not that kind, despite what I've sensed on the other side of some invisible veil all my life. It's a shared psychosis or something.

Stop thinking about fucking monsters. Focus on Gerard so you can get back out there and lie to him.

The more I think about his wounded face, the more I feel like an asshole. He's trying to connect. I don't deserve him. I should break things off now before he gets more attached.

Except it'll break his heart. He's had several shitty relationships. His last two girlfriends cheated on him. And before that, there was Julia, the love of his life who died in a car accident.

He'd told me on more than one occasion that I was the first person to make him happy since her. I don't want to take that away. But I also can't let anyone in because one night he's going to fall asleep beside me. It'll happen whether I want it or not.

I'll end up in his head, or his dreams. I'll see his darkest secrets or shames and that'll be it.

Once you've seen the worst parts of a person, the darkness they hide from everyone, sometimes even themselves, it's hard to see them as they truly are again. The darkness swallows everything else forever.

I wipe the tears from my eyes, freshen up in the mirror, and head back out to join Gerard, finalizing my cover story as I approach the table.

But he isn't there. I sit, figuring maybe he went to the bathroom.

The waiter comes over and hands me an envelope. "Your date said he had an emergency and to give you this. He's taken care of the bill."

"Thanks," I say, taking the envelope.

Did he have an emergency call from work? I'm thinking he'd at least text me if so. That's faster than writing a letter and leaving it with the waiter.

I get up from the table and head out, opening the envelope as I approach the front doors.

I REALLY TRIED, *Delaney.*

I'll be here when you're ready to actually talk.

Just don't make me wait too long.

— Gerard.

I GET INTO MY CAR, torn between being hurt that he left and grateful that he's given me an easy way to break things off. Now I never have to have The Conversation.

Still, the ache is surprisingly deep.

My phone rings.

Almost expecting it to be Gerard, I pick it up without even looking at the name.

"Del! I need help!"

It's Anika.

TWENTY-NINE

Delaney

Anika asked me to meet her at the Starlite All Nite near her house, a retro 50s diner with shiny metal surfaces and a few era versions of campy futuristic flourishes. Makes me think of *The Jetsons*.

I pull up just after eleven and see Anika sitting alone in a booth. She's wearing sweats, a long pink tee and a denim jacket, as if in a rush to flee her apartment. There's a denim backpack beside her.

I go inside, wondering what's wrong.

I sit at her booth and see her eyes are ringed and red, puffy. A glass of milk and a plate of French toast with scrambled eggs are sitting barely touched in front of her.

"What's wrong?"

"He came to my apartment, demanding money. He threatened my sister."

"No."

"Yes. And I … I don't feel safe there anymore."

"I'm going to take care of it." I pull out my phone and am about to call him.

She stops me. "Whatever you were going to do, he knows about it."

"What do you mean?"

"He told me to call you off of him or else he'd kill my sister, and her little girl."

"Fuck. That rat went and told him."

"I don't know what to do, Del."

"Don't worry, we'll figure something out. How long do you have?"

"He said I had another day."

"I'll get you the money. I've got some favors I can call."

"You … you don't even know me."

"No, but I've been down before. And I know how it feels to have your back against the wall. I can't let him hurt you or your family."

She's sobbing now, face in her hands.

"It's going to be okay." I reach out to touch her.

Anika can't see me, but still she flinches the moment my hand reaches her.

She looks up and meets my eyes. "Sorry. I'm … I'm on edge."

Something feels off. Can she sense my ability? I still can't shake the feeling that she's hiding something.

I stare at Anika, trying to see through her mask of pain, if there's someone or something else in there. But honestly, I sense more from Seb.

She shakes her head, tears falling. "I don't know what to do. Or how he got into my house. I'm scared to go back."

"You can stay with me."

"Are you sure?"

"Don't worry." I lay down some cash for her meal. "Let's get out of here."

~

I FILL up my air mattress, lay it on my bedroom floor, and dress it with fresh linens.

"You can take the bed. I'll sleep down here."

"No, I'm fine with an air mattress."

"If you sleep down here, my cat won't leave you alone. I'd sleep on the couch, but it's about as comfortable as a desk."

Anika looks at Pumpkin, sitting on the air mattress and glaring up at her.

"Can I pet him?"

"Not if you like keeping the blood *in* your veins."

She laughs. "Ah, so he's not a good kitty?"

"No, he's an asshole."

She laughs more.

Pumpkin turns his back to me, makes a couple of circles before plopping down on my pillow. As if to say, *Yeah, I understood, and fuck you.*

"Really? Gotta get hair on my pillow?"

I take it out from under him. He hisses before making a few more turns and getting comfortable on my blanket.

"If you want to shower, it's in there. I need to check on my neighbor."

"Okay," she says, "thank you again."

I go to the living room and stall until I hear the shower running. I look inside the bedroom and see her backpack on the floor.

I move quickly, rifling through it. Clothes on top, her wallet, a phone and charger … and another burner.

I turn it on. No passcode required, and see one number.

I memorize the digits, then slide the phone back into

her backpack. I feel around and find six large bottles, most filled with painkillers. An intent-to-sell amount.

What the fuck?

The bottle gives me a rush of memories — a scumbag-looking guy I've never seen. His pills, not hers. Why does she have them? He her dealer? Are these the missing drugs?

I get another image, of Anika swallowing the pills.

She's an addict.

Of course.

And then, under the bottles of pills, my hand falls on a familiar shape — a gun.

Fuck.

I grab the weapon, remove the bullets, and return the gun to her backpack.

I drop the bullets in my jacket, put everything else back as it was, and get the hell out of my room.

I USUALLY PUT my gun on my nightstand or somewhere close by while home. For now, I'll keep it in my back holster, hidden by a loose shirt and jacket.

My mind is racing, trying to make sense of the drugs and gun. I get the weapon. Anika's running scared. But there's no good reason for that amount of drugs. Even for an addict.

Maybe the guy I saw the flashes of was Jay's dealer. Maybe it's his stash. Though, I have no doubt my flash of her using wasn't an error. She's an addict. And, in my experience, you can't ever trust an addict.

I still feel an overwhelming instinct to protect her. That's only part of the reason I invited her to stay with me. I'll dip into her dreams, find out what she's hiding tonight.

I only hope I don't make the darkness inside her worse. I'm not sure if I can handle another death on my conscience.

I leave my place and knock on Seb and Ned's door.

Seb answers, wearing sweats and a tank top, his impressive muscles on ample display. "Hey, Del. How's it going?"

"Got a few minutes?"

"Sure, come on in."

He invites me into his kitchen, chicken and rice on the stove. "Just got home from work, eating late."

"How's Ned?" I take a seat at the bar.

"Back still hurting. He was doing better, then he went and twisted it again. He's asleep."

"Ah, sorry." I look around, surprised Brandy isn't begging for belly rubs. She's probably in bed with Ned.

"So, what's going on?"

I update Seb on everything that happened with Anika, leaving out the parts about the demons and flashes. Seb knows I'm psychic, but nothing beyond that. My father and Brother Clarence are the only ones who know what other things I'm capable of.

"Basically, I don't know if I can trust her. And I'm sure she's an addict. Any advice?"

"You asking about what to do about the gangster or her drug addiction?"

"I don't know. I just needed to get out of the house to think."

"Have you asked Gerard? Might be able to help, seeing he's a cop."

"We're not exactly on the best of terms."

"Oh no, what happened?"

I tell him about dinner.

"Why don't you just open up to him?"

"You wouldn't understand."

"Try me."

It would feel nice to tell someone this thing that's been weighing me down. Seb's a good guy. And, since we're not super close, it's not like I fear his judgment.

"I'm going to tell you something that'll sound crazy."

"I respond to fires, accident scenes, and shootings. I see crazy on most days ending in Y."

"This is next-level nuts. Like supernatural shit."

"More than you being psychic?"

"Do you believe in psychic abilities?"

"Like I said, I see crazy, unexplainable things all the time. I have a very open mind. Besides, I know you found that girl when nobody else could. Fortune tellers and psychic hotlines might be bullshit, but I do believe that some people can tap into things science can't yet explain. Like you."

I wonder how much he knows about my childhood, the "healing" that Father had me doing. We've never discussed it, but any Google search of my father or my birth name would deliver all sorts of crazy stories, most of which I don't remember enough to know if they're true.

"Okay, you want to know the real reason I don't let Gerard sleep over?"

"Of course." He turns off the stove and shovels generous portions onto two plates. "But first you have to try my mother's recipe."

I'm surprised to find myself hungry and dig in to the steaming spicy chicken and rice.

"Damn, this is good."

"Hers was even better, God rest her soul. Carry on." Seb sits across from me and starts eating.

"Sometimes when I touch someone I get flashes of

emotions, or memories. I can't quite read their minds, but I see things they probably wouldn't want me to."

"For real? Have you ever done it to me?"

"I try to avoid touching people I know for exactly that reason. Sometimes when you've hugged me, I've sensed you were mad or sad, but no specifics. I try to break away before seeing too much."

I don't tell Seb that something about him makes me want to stay away. I don't see any sign of disbelief or suspicion. But he's looking, waiting without judgment for me to continue.

"Anyway, it's worse when I'm sleeping next to someone. I end up in their dreams. And I can't control what they show me. I'm trapped, forced to see the darkest things."

"Like what?"

"Something they did in their past and are ashamed of, a dark fear, or maybe an ugly fantasy from their subconscious. But once inside them, I see it. And, on one occasion, I was sure me being in their head only made the darkness worse — fed it."

"What happened?"

"His name was Charles, my college boyfriend. My one true love, if that's not too corny. The first and last person I ever let in. He was, by all accounts, a happy, well-adjusted person before I fell asleep next to him. He was smart, funny, and on his way to doing big things in the world. And then I saw his darkness — an obsession with hurting his twin sister, Claire."

"Like a fantasy?"

"I don't think he really wanted to hurt her. He loved his sister. She was one of my best friends, and definitely his. I don't know the origin of his darkness, just that he had these awful thoughts about her. They were sexual and some involved hurting her."

"Damn. And you're sure he wasn't some closet deviant?"

"I honestly don't think he was. Anyway, I tried to ignore it. I wasn't going to stay over at his place anymore because I felt like I'd invaded his privacy. But I wanted to know more, to know if there was something there, maybe from their past. Or maybe a trusted person in his life did something to him and it was manifesting in these thoughts about his sister. I wanted to know if the man I loved was a monster, or if this was his psyche's way of dealing with trauma."

I wish Seb drank alcohol because I could use a glass of something.

I ask for one of his near beers and he gets me one. I take a drink. Tastes like piss, but it'll have to do.

I continue. "So, I started staying over, each night seeing more and more. Eventually his thoughts grew even darker, into torture and murder."

"Oh shit."

"I couldn't ask him about these dreams, of course. *Hey, I just spied on you in your sleep. Mind explaining?* He became withdrawn and started avoiding me. Avoiding everybody. Not going to class, and nowhere near his sister. He blew me off whenever I called, saying he wasn't feeling good. Part of me thought maybe he knew I'd been in his head. Maybe he was ashamed and was pushing me away. I let him be."

I need a moment before I continue.

"A few weeks went by, then Claire called and asked me to check on him. She was out of town. So I went to his place and found him in his bathtub with his wrists slit."

Seb is blinking back tears.

"He left a suicide note, addressed to me and Claire.

I don't know what's wrong with me. I've been having these very dark, scary thoughts. I thought I was going to hurt someone I love. Please, forgive me.

"So he killed himself before he hurt anyone, instead of getting help?"

"Yes, but here's the part I hate to admit. Claire couldn't deal with his death. She asked me to take care of his belongings. And while I was packing stuff and deciding who to give what, I found a diary. And here's the thing — he didn't start having those dark thoughts until I went into his head."

"What do you mean?"

"Those thoughts might have been there, but they were buried in his subconscious. His diaries before that first night were totally normal. But then they grew progressively worse. The thoughts seeped into his waking life until he became obsessed. Until he was actively fantasizing about hurting and killing his sister. And ... he didn't want these thoughts. He kept trying to purge them with drugs and alcohol. But they kept getting worse and he was afraid of what he was becoming. Hated himself and what he might do. You see, Seb? Something about me being in his head fed the darkness, brought it into the light. *I'm* the reason he's dead. I killed him."

"You don't know that."

"I do, though. I can't explain how, but I know. And I can't ever do that to anyone again."

"I'm so sorry," Seb says, going to put his hand in mine before stopping short.

Then, realizing what he's done, he goes to touch my hand anyway.

I pull away. "It's okay. I understand. This is why I don't tell anyone. Once someone knows, they can never be completely comfortable with me."

"Is there anything I can do? About this or about Anika, or anything?"

"No, I just needed someone to talk to, I guess. Thanks for listening."

"Wish I could help."

"You did."

He's wiping tears and I feel stupid for having unloaded all of this on him. Nobody should be burdened with the curse of *me*.

"For what it's worth, I still think you should reach out to Gerard about Rufus. He might be able to help. He's a beat cop and Rufus might be on vice, but he can probably reach out to someone."

So can Dusty.

"Maybe. I'll think about it."

"You shouldn't go it alone, Del. I've stitched up enough people on the south side to know what guys like Rufus are capable of."

"I know."

"As for Anika, if she ODs, you can give her something for it." He gets up, goes to another room, then brings back a needle and a bottle of Naloxone. He explains how to administer it, and that time is of the essence.

I thank him, for both the medicine and for listening. I offer to help clean up, but Seb says he's got it.

It's awkward for us both since he usually hugs me when I go, but now he's probably afraid of what I'll see inside him, or what I might unleash.

I should never have told him.

THIRTY

Anika

Anika is sitting in the shower, letting the hot water pummel her as she struggles with what Rufus asked her to do.

Del has been so kind. She can't kill her.

BUT IF YOU DON'T, HE WILL MURDER Chelsea AND Emery.

How the hell do I kill someone who hasn't even hurt me? Del hasn't done anything to me.

SHE LIED WHEN YOU MET.

SHE'S USING YOU TO GET INFORMATION.

SHE KNOWS WHAT YOU DID TO JAY.

I didn't do anything to Jay.

STOP PRETENDING. YOU MIGHT NOT REMEM-BER, BUT YOU STILL KNOW WHAT HAPPENED.

No, she doesn't. And that's the problem. Anika doesn't remember what happened to Jay or Frankie. But thanks to that video, now she has a story.

She never should've watched it.

Now she knows the truth. That she isn't alone in her body. There's something inside her. That isn't a friendly inner voice. It's something far deadlier, infesting Anika's every thought.

How do you get away from something that lives inside you?

Did you kill Jay?

HE WAS HURTING US. HE NEEDED TO GO.

The confirmation of his death stirs a sickness in Anika's gut, a pain in her heart. Not only because he's gone, but that *she* had something to do with it.

DON'T MOURN HIM. HE WAS AN ABUSIVE FUCK. WE'RE BETTER OFF WITHOUT HIM.

What did you do?

IT'S BEST YOU DON'T REMEMBER. YOU'RE SAFE NOW. OR YOU WILL BE … ONCE WE TAKE CARE OF THE WOMAN.

I'm not going to kill her.

YOU DON'T NEED TO DO ANYTHING. JUST LET ME DO THE WORK.

No!

YOU WANT TO KEEP YOUR SISTER AND HER KID ALIVE, DON'T YOU?

She's working on a solution. She'll figure something out.

THE ONLY THING SHE'S TRYING TO FIGURE OUT IS WHAT HAPPENED TO JAY. WHAT DO YOU THINK SHE'LL DO ONCE SHE FINDS OUT? THINK SHE'S GOING TO LET YOU GO? OR WILL SHE HAVE YOU ARRESTED FOR HIS MURDER?

I can't kill someone.

SHE IS NOT A GOOD PERSON. TRUST ME. SHE ISN'T WHAT YOU THINK SHE IS.

SHE'S DONE BAD THINGS.

ASK HER ABOUT HER FATHER.

TRUST ME, YOU WILL BE DOING THE WORLD A FAVOR.

Anika can no longer take it.

She gets out of the bath, dries off, then goes to her backpack, grabs one of the bottles and takes three pills to silence the hell inside her.

Then one more to fall asleep.

THIRTY-ONE

Delaney

I get back to find Anika sleeping soundly in my bed. Pumpkin found the pillow I'd thrown on top of my dresser and is fast asleep on it.

Asshole.

I grab another one from my closet, hang my jacket, and head back into the living room to unwind with a beer while working to calm my nerves.

I can't stop worrying about Anika's dreams. What if I do what I did to Charlie and make things worse?

How much worse can things get, though, if there's really a monster inside her? I need to find out, even if I don't know what I can do about it.

Maybe Father can come up with something else? He did seem to be thinking before he drifted off again.

I also can't stop thinking about the supposed monster inside him. The one I'd driven from the mayor. If that's true, how long did it stay there? And how much was it responsible for the lies and thievery, his eventual fall before going to jail?

I've hated him for so long. But now I have to reconsider

the man I thought I knew. I've so much rage for how he'd made me the centerpiece of his church as some Miracle Child — something he did long before there was any monster inside of him.

But I didn't hate him as a child. I believed in the cause, even if I was uncomfortable with the attention and how I usually felt after healing one of the flock.

The hate came when I saw him as the charlatan he later became. If that wasn't him, but in reality a monster forcing him to do these things, have I loathed my father for nothing?

I grab another beer and sit at my kitchen counter on my laptop, tempted to research Brother Clarence, use one of the databases to find out where he's been these past few years.

But I'm suddenly too tired, so I finish my beer off and head to bed.

Pumpkin is on my bed, on the new pillow.

I swear *he* has a monster inside him! I pick him up and drop him at the end of the air mattress where he turns in circles, annoyed at me.

I shake his fur off my pillow, then grab the other one from my dresser and throw it on the ground beside me.

I pat it.

He comes to the pillow and gets on, lying down next to me.

I pet his head and he purrs, rubbing his head against me.

Sometimes he can be sweet.

I close my eyes, hoping sleep takes me soon so I can see what's going on in Anika's head.

~

I'M STANDING outside Jay's apartment.

I hear him screaming inside, "Where the hell is it?"

I hear Anika cry, "I don't know."

"Don't you fucking lie to me! These people do not fuck around."

"I swear, I don't know."

I hear things being tossed. He's looking for his stash, which means he didn't take off with it.

I open the door. It's unlocked, though I'm not sure if it really would have been.

I go inside and close it behind me.

There's stuff everywhere — the house torn apart. Jay looks scared. His hair is a greasy mess and his eyes are bloodshot.

He's drunk, but … also something else. Judging from his erratic, frantic movements and the way his eyes are darting around in paranoid glances, I'm guessing coke.

Anika is fetal on the couch, afraid to move and crying.

"Where is it?" he screams again.

Anika is sobbing uncontrollably.

She says something that surprises me, and apparently Jay. "I'm sorry."

"What?" He turns to her.

"I'm sorry. I didn't mean to."

"What did you do?" Jay runs up to Anika on the couch, grabs her by the shoulders, and starts shaking her hard.

I want to intervene, but I can't change the past, and any action might alert Anika's dreaming self to my presence.

I'm a silent observer of history.

"I didn't mean to!" Anika cries again.

"What didn't you mean to do?"

She can't look at him.

"Tell me!"

"I left the car unlocked. The trunk was open when I came out of the store, and the bag was gone."

"You were supposed to put it in your closet, goddammit! Why didn't you go straight home?"

"I'm sorry!"

"Fuck!" Jay screams, sitting at the end of the couch and putting his head in his hands. "Rufus is gonna kill me."

Anika sits up and puts an arm on his shoulder, trying to comfort him. "Talk to him. I'm sure you can work something out."

He turns to Anika. "There was more than fifteen grand's worth of pills in there!"

"Why did you even give it to me, then? Why didn't you keep it in your place?"

"Are you fucking blaming me?"

"No, but … it's not my fault!"

"You left your fucking car unlocked! You didn't do the *one thing* I asked — just take it home. How fucking stupid are you?"

"I'm not stupid!" Anika yells, surprisingly forceful.

Something shifts in her face. It's only a moment, then her voice changes, ever so slightly. Less fearful, more assertive.

"This is your fault. *You* fucked up. I'm tired of you always blaming me."

He stares at Anika as if she smacked him. "What did you say?"

She's just as surprised, her eyes wide and mouth agape, speechless.

Jay backhands her and something goes bright in his eyes. A look I've seen too many times — a glee abusers get before unleashing.

He grabs her by the hair, about to hit her again.

She meets his eyes and laughs. "Do it, you pussy!"

His eyes widen.

Fuck.

And again. Anika looks surprised.

Jay smacks her even harder.

I want to turn away, but I can't. I have to see how this plays out.

Anika clocks him in the eye with a balled-up fist.

He screams.

She scrambles away from the couch, running.

"You fucking bitch!"

Now he's chasing her.

Anika throws herself into the bathroom and slams the door.

He's pounding hard on the wood. "Open this fucking door, right fucking now!"

Anika is sobbing on the other side. "I didn't mean to, I swear."

"Open the fucking door, Anika, or else!"

I can hear the absolute terror in her voice even though all I see is Jay banging on the door, muscles in his shoulders and neck bulging beneath his tank top.

"Open the fucking door, Anika," Jay keeps repeating while pacing, getting louder each time.

I'm shocked that no one is hearing this. That nobody's called the police.

Jay stops pacing and goes at the door with both fists, pounding over and over. "Open the fucking door, open the fucking door, open the fucking door!"

Anika's bawling. "Go away. I'm gonna call the cops."

He looks back at the couch, sees her phone on the coffee table, and laughs. "Your phone is out here, you dumb cunt. Open the door now or I swear to God I'll fucking kill you."

He starts banging again, harder, faster, and louder, the veins on his neck taut, his face burning crimson with rage.

"Open the door!"

The doorknob unlocks.

Jay stands back, readying his fists.

The door swings open.

Anika is crouched on the floor, looking as though she's passed out. I see something dark, like the shadow of a person with glowing white eyes.

It opens its mouth and says, "You're going to what?"

He screams and turns to run.

The thing grabs Jay, yanks his body into the bathroom and hurls it into the tub.

Then the shadow is on him, opening its mouth to rows of razor teeth the color of midnight.

He screams as it lunges, parting its jaw wide and gnashing Jay's face away from his skull. What's left looks like a watermelon with bones.

I yelp.

The dark thing turns toward me, somehow seeing me through space and time.

My eyes flit back to Jay's body, with half his face gone, his skull and brain a gory mess. The image floods my mouth with vomit.

The dark thing turns away from me, then devours Jay's thrashing, screaming form, leaving nothing behind except the blood coating the tub.

I step backwards, ready to wake up.

Wake up, I command myself.

But I'm not going anywhere.

The shadow thing turns and looks at me.

And in a leathery, ancient voice it says, "*Well, hello, Delaney.*"

THIRTY-TWO

Delaney

"No, I'm not the monster of your childhood."

"How do you know what I'm thinking?" I ask as it stares at me.

It's a shadow, slightly taller than me, with substance, layers of darkness within darkness, constantly moving, flowing like viscous matter. Like the monster that lived inside the mayor.

"You're in our head. And I can see inside yours," it says with a menacing smile.

The monster takes a shambling step toward me, moving in a stop motion hiccup.

"Get out of her!" I shout, hoping for authority.

It laughs, a sickly, choking laugh. *"You've got no power here, The Great Delaney."*

It knows my childhood name. How?

"You already know how."

Another step forward.

I stand firm, refusing to back down.

Fuck this monster trying to scare me. I'm not afraid of you!

I hope you heard that!

"Indeed, I did. Such a brave child."

It's inches away from me. A cold chill runs through my soul. Even if I'm not physically here in Anika's head, I can feel its body too close. Breathing cold putrescence in my face.

I gag and it laughs again.

We're no longer in Jay's apartment. And Anika's gone.

We're in … my childhood home.

How?

"I'm in your dream now, your memories."

I try to wake up so I can get this monster out of my head. I can usually think of something to snap me out of a dream, but I can't think of anything that'll bring me out of this one.

"Such a lovely place you have here." It's walking away, moving down the hallway toward my old bedroom.

"Stay out of there!"

It stops at the sound of a voice I haven't heard in forever. *Mother.*

"Oh, what's upstairs?" It turns and climbs to where my parents are talking.

"Stay away from her!" I shout, racing up the steps to stop it.

I reach for its shoulder to spin it around.

My hand goes through the monster and begins to burn.

I yank my hand back, screaming in agony. I look down at my hand and arm, expecting to see burn marks or worse, but there's no sign of injury. And now there's no pain.

I follow the monster upstairs.

It's in my parents' room, standing in the corner, watching them argue.

I stare at my mother, so much younger than I

remember her. So much prettier, despite her sorrowful eyes.

She's crying. "You have to stop, Ted. There's something wrong with her."

Who are they talking about?

"They're talking about you, Dearie. But you know that already."

Something about this conversation feels so oddly familiar, like I've heard it before, but that's impossible. I'm not in the bedroom. And I certainly don't remember this.

Then again, most of my childhood is a mystery.

When is this?

"She's fine!" Father is adamant.

"She's not. Our daughter hasn't been right for some time. You have to know that."

"What is your problem with her? Are you jealous of your own daughter? That all the parishioners love her and ignore you?"

Mother glares at him. "You know I don't give a damn about what they think of me. Though, I sure wish you did."

"You need to ignore the naysayers, stop letting your vanity infect your head."

He pushes his index finger against her skull, hard. It looks like it hurts. I've never seen my father demonstrate violence. I wonder if the monster is inside him already.

The monster laughs. *"Oh, it's not in your father ... not yet."*

What the hell do you know?

"Apparently, more than you. Stay tuned, Dearie. You're about to remember everything."

I don't want this. I want to wake up!

"You don't want to know why your dear mother left? Say the word and I'll wake you both. Or, you can stay for the truth."

I stare at the smiling shadow, hands folded, awaiting an answer.

I continue to watch as the past unspools before me.

"These people don't love her. They worship her. It's scary. Creepy, even. And you're living vicariously through their adulation of her!"

Father smacks her across the face.

I'm filled with rage. I want to put myself between them, protect my mother, hug her and swear that I'll never let him hurt her again.

But I'm powerless.

Mother stares at him, refusing her tears. A much stronger woman than I remember.

"You can hit me like a coward, but I refuse to be silenced." Her voice is sharp, shaking as if she's using all her restraint not to scream. Still, civility doesn't lessen the blunt force trauma of her words. "And I refuse to let my daughter attend any more of your sermons until she sees a therapist."

"Those shrinks are agents of the Devil! I trust in a higher power."

She gets in his face, jaw clenched, almost daring him to strike her again. "You listen to me, Ted. If you bring our daughter back to your sermons, I will leave and take her with me. Try and stop me, and I'll claim you've been abusing us both. I'll go to the police, then the press. I'll go to anyone who will listen and bring this church to its knees. Do you understand me?"

Father stares at her, stunned.

I've never seen him speechless. Or nearly this mad. He's shaking, and looks like he's going to hurt her.

Instead, he walks out of the bedroom and slams the door.

Mother collapses onto the bed and finally allows herself to weep.

I'm crying too as I stand here helplessly watching, unable to do anything.

Is this why she left?

Why didn't she take me with her like she threatened?

I look over to the shadow monster, staring past me and smiling.

I turn, trying to figure out what it's looking at, and why the hell it's smiling. What does it know that I don't? What does it see?

And then I notice, the closet door slowly opening.

What's happening?

And then I walk out. The thirteen-year-old me.

Why don't I remember this?

Younger Me is walking slowly toward Mother, eyes watering.

She's still sobbing, doesn't yet see me.

My heart thrums in my throat. A cold dread blended with déjà vu washes through me.

What happened? Why don't I remember this?

Mother starts when she notices me. "Honey! Wh-what are you doing in here?"

She sits up, wiping her tears. Younger Me walks over, opens her arms and pulls Mother into a warm embrace.

Why the hell don't I remember this?

"I'm sorry you were fighting over me."

She puts her head on Younger Me's chest. "It's okay, honey. It's not your fault. We're going to get you help. I promise."

"But I don't need help, Mother."

She tries to pull away to look up and argue otherwise, but Younger Me is holding her head tight.

Let go of her!

Mom cries out, "Del, let go of me."

"I'm sorry, Mommy. But I can't do that."

"Del?" Mom cries out as Younger Me holds her tighter, too tight.

Tears are streaming down my younger face.

What the hell is happening?

I run to pull Younger Me off of Mother, but the moment I touch her, I bounce back to where I was standing.

"Del!"

Younger Me opens her mouth. Big and wide, the dark teeth inside.

Oh God, no!

Her face shifts into that of the monster inside her — inside Younger Me — and she bites down, tearing into Mother's skull.

"No!"

We're back in darkness. My childhood home is gone, and only nothing surrounds me.

I did it.

I killed my mother.

Or the monster inside me did, when I couldn't stop it.

"Some part of you wanted her dead or you wouldn't have let it happen." The monster moves closer. *"So, yes, you killed your mother. How do you feel?"*

I can only see it because of its white eyes and glistening teeth.

"And now you know what really happened to your mother. You're welcome."

I reach out to tear its fucking head from its body.

My hands slip around its throat, but the monster isn't scared.

Instead, it smiles. *"Wakey, wakey, The Great Delaney."*

I open my eyes, gasping.

And Anika's hands are around my throat.

THIRTY-THREE

Delaney

I gasp, my legs kicking at her helplessly, arms thrashing.

Then I remember the gun.

I manage to twist around and grab the weapon. I don't want to shoot Anika, but if I don't do something, the Monster inside her will kill me.

I aim the gun at Anika.

She turns just in time to see what I'm doing.

I fire but she knocks the gun from my hand, back under my dresser, too far out of reach.

She lets go of my neck, so I punch her in the jaw. It's enough to knock her back off of me.

I scramble, trying to get back to the gun. I don't want to kill her, but fuck if I'm gonna let that thing end me.

I remember my father's warning. It'll go inside me if I kill her.

Shit!

I leap to my feet, surprised to find my hands burning bright.

Maybe I can get it out of her? But if I do that, does that mean it'll jump in me?

I remember what Father said about the monster jumping in him. But that's not what happened — it jumped into me instead, then hid for years.

Memories spill forth — him getting the demon out of me. Father has the power, or curse. He took my monster so I would no longer suffer.

Then he and Brother Clarence must've cleaned the mess, figured out a way to hide my murder.

Anika's clearly frightened.

Her eyes widen as I approach.

She rushes past me, into the living room. Throws the front door open and races out.

Seb is standing there.

She shoves him, straight off the fourth floor.

I scream.

Anika leaps off the fourth floor, too.

I race to the rail and peer over in time to see her bouncing to her feet, then racing into the night. Seb hits the pavement next to the pool, face first.

Shit!

I race to the stairwell then down the steps, praying he's okay. But I see he's not moving as I hit the ground floor, blood pooled around his face.

No, no, no, no!

I run over and fall to the ground.

My hands are still glowing bright, burning hot.

Can I … can I heal him?

I have to try.

I slowly roll him onto his side, see his face shattered at the cheekbone.

I turn away before I vomit, then reach down and feel for a pulse. Faint, but there.

I have to try something, so I lay my hands on the back

of his head and focus. Close my eyes and ask God to please not let him die.

I flash back on the dozens of people I've healed over the years. Not those whose monsters I pulled out, not that I can remember them yet, but I can recall the sick and frail I somehow, sometimes, managed to heal.

I focus, trying to remember how I did it, and what I thought while it was happening.

But that doesn't work, so I keep thinking, *Please don't die.*

Please don't die.

Please don't die.

Please don't die.

Please don't die.

I see something inside him, a memory of him running. But it doesn't make sense. He's on all fours.

He's a dog.

No, not a dog.

A …

His body moves in my hands, groaning as he turns over to face me.

His face is knitting itself, but also shifting, bones moving beneath the flesh, nose protruding.

At first I think it's me healing him, but no, Seb's face's is shifting. His nose becomes a snout. His teeth canine. Dark hair sprouting all over his face.

Holy fuck, he's a werewolf!

He's staring up at me, flesh healed and his face half wolf.

I'm stunned and unable to hide my expression.

He feels his face as it's finally returning to human form.

He sits up, embarrassed, maybe afraid.

I point at him. "You're a fucking werewolf?"

He smiles sheepishly. "Well, I guess we've both got secrets."

We stare at each other for a long moment of silence before we both burst into laughter.

I help him up.

"Does … does Ned know?"

"Of course. I don't keep secrets from my loved ones," he teases. "What happened? I … could've sworn I saw something dark inside of her when she hit me."

"She has a monster inside her."

"A *what?*"

"Come upstairs, I've got a lot to tell you. I hope you don't mind, but I need a fucking drink."

"No problem."

I TELL HIM EVERYTHING, pouring out my soul and even crying on his shoulder.

"I can't believe I killed my mother."

"You didn't do it. The monster did."

"Yeah, but Anika's monster said it wouldn't have happened if I didn't want it to on some level. And then … my father, who've I've spent all my adult life hating, took the monster inside. I don't know why I don't remember any of it, but he let me believe he was the one who drove my mother off for all these years. He was protecting me from what I did."

I break down, full-on sobbing into his chest. I don't normally like contact, but now I need someone to hug me.

"I feel so fucking awful. I have to apologize to him."

"You can," Seb says. "But what are you going to do about Anika?"

"No idea. I don't know how to defeat the monster."

"You think it'll come back after you?"

"No. I ... I think it's scared to be in me. I think it wants to stay inside her."

"Why?"

"My father might have answers, but I don't know."

I look at the clock. It's way too late to hit the nursing home. "I'll have to wait for tomorrow."

"I want you to come with me," Seb says.

"What?"

"Sleep at our place. We have a guest room. Just in case she comes back."

"You sure?" I say, wiping tears from my eyes.

"Yes."

"Oh, shit. I need to see if Pumpkin is okay."

I race to my room.

Pumpkin is fast asleep on my pillow.

"Asshole," I say, though I'm glad he's not hurt.

I grab my gun and some clothes before returning to Seb's. "Okay, ready for the sleepover."

"Wait a second. You're not gonna be jumping into *our* dreams or anything, are you?"

"Not unless we're sleeping in the same room. Why, got more secrets?"

"Only that I sometimes eat cats."

I stare at him, rolling my eyes.

"No, not really. Come on. We've got a big day tomorrow."

"We've?"

"You think I'm gonna let you fight a monster on your own?"

"I can handle a monster."

"Not saying you can't, but friends don't let friends fight monsters alone."

"You're so fucking corny," I say.

THIRTY-FOUR

Anika

Anika stumbles into her apartment, shaken and crying as she makes her way to the nightstand where she'd left one of her bottles.

She goes to the bathroom, hardly able to look in the mirror. But she still can't believe what happened. She saw the thing on the video killing Jay, but still doesn't remember doing it. Some part of her had hoped it was video editing. No way a monstrous thing like that could be living inside her.

And yet it was. This time she saw it. Even though Anika had no control over her body when it emerged and left her standing there helpless.

She stares in the mirror, searching for some sign of it.

She's in her pajamas, her hair a mess, skin pale and eyes bloodshot, but there's no hint of the monster inside her.

Anika looks closer, thinking she'll see something in her eyes, a dark swirl swimming around, or *something*.

"What are you?"

The thing, whatever it is, speaks in her head. That inner voice she'd always thought was some facet of herself, though now she understands that it clearly is not.

I AM A PART OF YOU.

"Bullshit! You are *not* a part of me!"

YOU CALLED ME EDWIN BECAUSE YOU DIDN'T KNOW WHAT ELSE TO CALL ME.

"Edwin was my bear!"

AND YOUR 'IMAGINARY' FRIEND. ONLY I'M NOT SO IMAGINARY.

"Oh my God, I'm crazy!" Anika pops three pills into her mouth, leans under the faucet, turns on the sink, and swallows them down.

HEY, NOT TOO MANY. WE NEED TO DRIVE.

"Drive? And go where?"

ANYWHERE BUT HERE! NO WAY THAT BITCH WON'T RAT US OUT. THE COPS'LL BE HERE ANY MINUTE.

What the hell did you do? You tried to kill her! I didn't want to hurt her! I was going to let her figure out a way to take care of Rufus.

SHE KNOWS WHAT WE ARE. WE HAD TO DO SOMETHING.

You didn't have to try and kill her!

I DO WHATEVER I NEED TO DO TO KEEP US ALIVE!

BE GRATEFUL.

I COULD JUST LEAVE YOU.

Please, do!

YOU WILL DIE IF I DO. YOU CAN'T LIVE WITHOUT ME, ANIKA. WE ARE FORGED TOGETHER.

Anika stares in the mirror, tears streaming down her cheeks.

What do I do?

WE RUN.

Run where? And with what?

I'LL FIGURE IT OUT. FIRST, WE NEED CASH.

Anika laughs like a crazy person who's lost it all, save that last raw nerve of sanity.

Um, hello, I've been trying to get cash for like a week now!

WELL, NOW WE NO LONGER HAVE TO PLAY BY THE RULES, SO WE CAN GO STRAIGHT TO THE SOURCE.

What?

FIND RUFUS. TAKE HIS STASH.

Um, how?

I'LL TAKE CARE OF IT.

I don't even know where Rufus is. And he has guns. I don't even know how to use a gun.

I DON'T NEED GUNS. GET IN THE CAR.

Anika's body obeys even though she has no recollection of choosing to move.

And now she's in the car.

DRIVE.

Where?

WE WAITED OUTSIDE HIS PLACE ONCE WHEN JAY WENT TO PICK UP DRUGS.

I don't remember that.

I HAD TO ERASE A FEW MEMORIES SO YOU WOULDN'T.

You erased my memories?

I PROTECT YOU. ALWAYS HAVE, EVER SINCE YOU WERE LITTLE.

Anika doesn't want to believe any of this. It's all a nightmare she can't wake from. She wants to take the entire bottle of pills and never open her eyes again.

She's driving, praying that a cop won't pull her over.

One look, even before the pills kick in, and any cop would know she's on *something*.

ANIKA'S STANDING in front of Rufus's beachfront house.

Like most waterfront homes, his place is huge, stunning with large windows in the front, a circular driveway with luxury sports cars and motorcycles, a deck with a pool leading down to the beach. Easily worth a few million.

Lights are on despite the hour. There are people inside dancing to thrumming music. The party never stops at the dealer's place.

Some weird animal-like sense that Anika's never had before can feel Rufus inside the house.

In a back room.

She circles around to the rear.

No gate or guards or anyone else to stop her, even if they could.

Anika's body is filled with an adrenaline and a hunger that now belongs to her. She feels what the monster inside her feels as fear and terror subside with her doubts.

Her resistance is faded, her will trapped behind glass.

She walks onto the deck.

A trio of women and a wrinkled old man are hanging out in the hot tub.

"What the hell?" says the guy in a drugged or drunken slur.

She smiles seductively. "Here to see Rufus."

"Ah." The man points with a beer to an open sliding glass door.

She looks inside, sees him lying in bed, eyes closed, nude, getting blown by a blonde.

She enters the room and closes the door, followed by the curtain.

Rufus and the blonde both look up at Anika in disbelief.

He sits up, his erection still at full attention, confusion at war with his arousal. Part of him thinks she's here to fuck him, too. Anika can sense it, and will use that to her advantage.

She tells the blonde to get out.

The blonde looks at Rufus, who nods his approval.

The blonde grabs her dress, doesn't bother putting it on, and goes out to the deck, sliding the door shut behind her.

Rufus stares at Anika, smiling and licking his lips. "You come for this?"

He grabs his cock.

"Yes," she says, approaching the bed.

He lies back down.

She straddles him, feeling his erection against her pajamas.

Some part of her is aroused, and Anika's not sure if it's her or the monster.

"Close your eyes," she says, rubbing against him.

He obeys.

Please, don't, she begs. *I don't want to.*

OKAY, THEN WE DO IT THE OTHER WAY.

Her entire body shakes, something sloughing her off like a heavy coat hitting the floor.

The dark thing is out of her.

Her body falls back onto the bed, feeling heavy and sedated as she watches the monster descend upon Rufus, biting down on his dick.

He screams as it devours his stomach.

Anika can only watch, helpless to stop the bloodbath. She can't even close her eyes.

She hears the bedroom door open. Men screaming. The monster leaps toward them, more yelling.

Anika can only stare at her victim's dying eyes. His mouth opens, but whatever Rufus wants to say gets lost in one last gurgle of blood.

THIRTY-FIVE

Delaney

I wake to a soft knocking.

I sit up, reaching for my gun on the nightstand, momentarily forgetting where I am, and that the nightstand is on the other side of the bed.

"Del?" Seb says.

"Yeah, come in," I say, groggily.

He looks confused. "There's someone at the door for you."

"For me? Who?"

"Brother Clarence. You're right, he doesn't seem nearly as old as you said he is."

I get up, wondering two things. How he found me and if something is wrong with Father.

I leave my gun on the nightstand and head to the living room, where Brother Clarence is sitting on the couch opposite Ned. Both are drinking iced tea.

Brother Clarence doesn't stand. He raises his glass and greets me without a smile. "Delaney."

"What is it?" I ask, not sitting.

"Can we speak alone?" Brother Clarence is looking at Ned.

"Yes." Ned stands and motions toward the front door. Pats his lap and Brandy comes running over for a walk.

Seb looks at me: *You all right?*

I nod.

Seb follows Ned outside.

I sit in Ned's chair, bracing for whatever Brother Clarence has to tell me.

"You saw one, didn't you?"

"Saw what?" I know what he's referring to, but want to hear him say it.

"A monster. Your father told me you refused to leave well enough alone."

I nod.

"Where is it now?"

"No idea. The thing tried to kill me. I fired a gun and it ran off."

He steeples his fingers. "What happened?"

I tell Brother Clarence an abbreviated version of everything.

He nods. "So, you made contact. It's been in your head?"

"Yes."

"Then it isn't finished with you. You've been marked."

"What does that mean?"

"It already knows what you are. You opened the door by entering her mind. Now it will not rest until it's back inside you. You make for a far more powerful host than Anika."

"What do you mean it knows what I am?"

"You're not from this world, Delaney. You're from somewhere else."

"Okay, you're gonna need to be a little less cryptic, Brother Clarence."

"You're from another realm, one that exists outside of this one, parallel to it. You are a Sin-Eater. Born to devour sins. Born into servitude, someone who literally absorbs the sins of the wretched so they might gain entrance into The Beyond. Those filled with too much sin were banished to the In-Between, a limbo between worlds. But Sin-Eaters don't end up banished to the In-Between upon their death. They become corrupted Echoes of all the sins and darkness they ingested. Pure malevolence and insanity. Monsters. That's what you would have become."

I stare at Brother Clarence for a long moment, trying to see if he's fucking with me, but he isn't exactly known for his sense of humor.

"What?" I'm lucky I can manage after what he's lain at my feet.

"I brought you here, to this realm, to save you from that life. I found your parents in their darkest hour and gave them a child to raise. Your father was never supposed to let you heal anyone. But ... he believed God told him otherwise. He argued that the Lord led me to him, and that this was your Fate."

"And ... you believed him?"

"I was lost, too. In need of something to believe in, a mission. Your father is a very convincing man. And we are honor bound by Fate where I come from. You were special, and that was apparent from the moment I saw you. I was sure Fate had other plans for you, Delaney."

He's almost smiling as he says this, and I see a fondness in his eyes I've never noticed before. Brother Clarence has always been so calm and cool.

"I didn't see a threat to you in this realm. I didn't know the Echoes could come here."

He shrugged. Such a casual gesture almost looks wrong coming from Brother Clarence's body. "We didn't learn they'd infiltrated this realm until after you discovered one making a member of our congregation sick. You were healing a woman and it bled right out of her, so weak it died right there. I learned more about the Echoes and how to destroy them. You expelled them from their hosts, then your father and I killed them with potions and a spell. We told the parishioners it was holy water to destroy the demons. People had no idea what we were really battling. We were a small enough church from a tiny enough town, word never spread. You were our little secret."

His voice turned even more grave. "Until the mayor came to us. He was infected with an Ancient, so much more powerful than the others. The monster's name is Bez Kyehve. And … it leapt into you."

"What is an Ancient?"

"Some believe them to be Gods of the In-Between. Others think they're Gods from elsewhere who died and became the most powerful of Echoes."

"And it killed my mother?"

"So, you do remember?"

"Not all of it, no. The monster in Anika found my memories, showed them to me."

"You were able to control it for some time. I sought help from others in our world, but nobody knew how to extract it without killing you. We decided to leave it in, so long as you remained able to contain it. But something happened. It took over, and killed your mother."

"What happened after that?"

"We thought it was gone. The others had vanished so easily once out of their hosts, after we used the potions. I didn't realize it had transferred to your father. It controlled him for years, hiding right under my nose."

"So, Father wasn't what they said he was?"

"He was a good man when I knew him. It's hard to say if he changed after your mother died or after the monster entered him. I believe both events happened around the same time. But no, I don't believe your father was a bad man."

"What do I do about this … Echo? And how did it seem to know me?"

"We believe that some of them share a hive mind, though this isn't confirmed. Little about them is known in our circles."

"How did you know it was on to me?"

"It is my gift to sometimes see things, Delaney. That and my psychic connection to you and your father. This gift has failed me in the past, when the monster hid inside your father without my knowledge. But for dealing with the beast, I suggest this…"

Brother Clarence reaches into his coat pocket and withdraws a metal vial like the ones he and Father once used on the possessed.

"This is the last potion. My source vanished, and there's no way for me to return home. There are no more portals or people who can create them. At least no one who will help us.

"You need to extract it and kill it. But I'm no longer strong enough to help you.

The front door opens and Seb enters. "It's okay, I can help."

Brother Clarence looks at him, surprised he was able to hear our conversation. I am too.

Seb points to his ears. "I've got *really* good hearing. I'm a werewolf."

Brother Clarence looks from Seb to me, and he finally smiles. "Well, perhaps Fate still works through you,

Delaney."

"So, how do we find Anika and her monster?" I ask.

"That's the good news. She'll find you."

THIRTY-SIX

Anika

Anika is driving, her trunk stuffed with cash and drugs. All she wants to do is get out of town, cross the border into Canada, and never look back.

But the thing inside her won't let her leave just yet.

WE HAVE TO TIE UP LOOSE ENDS. WE ARE NOT SAFE IF SHE'S ALIVE.

"What if she's waiting?" Anika is staring into the rearview as if she can actually see the monster inside her. "What if she shoots me?"

SHE WON'T GET THE CHANCE.

"There has to be some other way." Anika vaguely remembers something from when the monster went into Del's mind. A blur, but still something suggesting that maybe Del would understand her situation, that if they could only reach an agreement, she would leave them be.

FINE. I'LL READ HER MIND AND SEE IF SHE'S REALLY AGREEING OR IF SHE PLANS TO BETRAY US.

"You promise?" Anika asks, still looking into the rearview.

I PROMISE.

~

ANIKA SITS in the darkness outside Delaney's apartment as rain pelts her car.

STOP STALLING.

"What if she's still awake?"

DON'T WORRY. WE'LL GET HER TO LISTEN. JUST GET OUT.

Anika resists, but she knows the thing inside her is only making an allowance until it tires of the game and finally takes over.

She's been trying little acts of defiance since last night, to see what control she could exert over the parasite. But it's impossible to trick something that's privy to her every thought.

THAT'S RIGHT. SO GET OUT NOW SO I DON'T HAVE TO BE THE BAD GUY.

I DON'T WANT TO MAKE YOU DO ANYTHING, ANIKA.

I'M NOT A PARASITE.

I PREFER TO SEE THIS AS A MUTUALLY BENEFI-CIAL RELATIONSHIP.

"So, you're a *symbiotic* parasite?"

It doesn't answer. Or seem to appreciate sarcasm.

She gets out of the car of her own free will and steps into the rain. Anika has a gun but doesn't bother taking it. It's not nearly as useful as the weapon inside her. Plus, she doesn't want Delaney to shoot her.

Anika hopes she can manage to work something out. What, she has no idea. Maybe she'll know by the time she reaches her apartment.

She still can't believe what the monster did to Rufus's men. It let the women go, except for the one who tried to stab her.

Anika passes the pool, remembering Del's neighbor, the one the monster shoved over the rail. She hopes he wasn't hurt too badly or killed.

She looks to the spot where he fell, as if it'll tell her his fate.

It doesn't.

Anika steps into the elevator, presses Del's floor, and watches the doors close.

She rides up, every nerve on edge. Her stomach wants to hurl, her throat is tight, and her heart has probably never beat harder.

The elevator doors slide open and Anika steps onto the walkway, avoiding the rain as it pours in at a driving slant. She sticks close to the wall and the doors to her left as she approaches Delaney's apartment.

She stops outside the doorway.

SOMETHING ISN'T RIGHT.

Anika is confused, a surge of heightened danger flooding her system.

What's not right?

SHE'S NOT ALONE.

GO! RUN!

Anika turns.

But then the door bursts open behind her.

THIRTY-SEVEN

Delaney

Seb races out the door and grabs Anika.

He's not in his wolf form, but he's assured us that he's still strong enough for the job. He doesn't want to turn into a werewolf here in our complex, where people might see him shift.

"Now!" he shouts.

I grab the holy water and unscrew the cap.

Brother Clarence is behind me, readying his part.

Anika is squirming, trying to break free, but Seb's hold is true.

I get the cap off and step forward, thrusting my arm out.

Anika slips free, spinning, and leaps over the rail, dropping four stories to the ground below to land on her feet.

Seb and I trade a glance.

I look down at the empty vial in my hand.

"Fuck! Now what?"

Seb leaps after Anika, changing into his wolf form, clothes ripping to shreds on the way.

I'm not dumb enough to leap four stories, so I turn to

Brother Clarence. "What the fuck do we do now? Sorry, didn't mean to say fuck. And there I go again … *Fuck!*"

"If you can drive it out, I can try the spell without the potion."

I race to the stairs, hoping Brother Clarence can keep up.

I push myself to take two and three steps at a time, praying I don't slip, fall, and break my neck. Time is melting away from me. Every second I'm not on the ground, I imagine the monster killing Seb, or getting away from him.

What if she took off and he's chasing her? There's no way we can both catch up to them.

I see Seb at the bottom of the stairwell, dragging Anika inside. It's weird to see him in his full werewolf form. His muscles are even more defined, his entire body coated in thick dark fur. His eyes are emerald green and extremely bright.

Anika's body is limp and she isn't moving.

"Did … did you kill her?" I ask as I reach them.

"Just knocked her out. Now what?"

"Lay your hands on her," Brother Clarence says as he reaches us. "I'll say the words that will expel this Echo back to the In-Between."

Seb has Anika in a headlock.

I approach, my hands glowing as if they have a mind of their own, ready for the work.

I lay my hands on her head. Anika's eyes shoot open. Brother Clarence starts chanting.

"Get out of her body!" My voice caroms off the stairwell and I hope it doesn't travel too far or draw any unwanted attention. I can't imagine what someone might think should they stumble upon what's happening.

Anika shakes her head, eyes desperate and pleading, "Please, don't do this. You'll kill me."

It hurts to see her so tormented.

"Ignore the Echo. Continue!" Brother Clarence restarts the spell.

"Get out of her body!" I shout again.

Anika screams, "Help! Rape!"

Seb covers her mouth.

She bites down.

He growls, squeezing her jaw so hard, I'm afraid he might puncture her skin.

I press harder and close my eyes, trying to focus, memories returning to times when I've done this before.

Energy moves from my hands and into Anika's body. She's spastic, grunting and crying and whining as if on fire.

"Get out of her body!"

Her body goes limp.

She's quiet.

Brother Clarence has stopped chanting.

Is it over?

I open my eyes and look at Anika. She's limp with her eyes closed.

I turn to see Brother Clarence.

"Is it done?" I ask.

He smiles. The Echo, instead of Brother Clarence. "Oh, this body is ... different."

"No!" I rush him, reaching for his head.

"Get out!"

Brother Clarence kicks me in the chest and sends me flying backwards into Seb and Anika, knocking all three of us to the ground.

Brother Clarence stares down, still smiling at us.

"Oh, this one has *many* secrets. A lot involving you, Delaney."

Seb pushes us off of him and leaps at Brother Clarence.

He dives out of the way, but not fast enough.

They tumble onto the stairs, Seb growling as he grabs Brother Clarence's head and slams it into the wall.

Brother Clarence leaps toward me.

Seb grabs him, pulling the man into a chokehold. He falls back onto the stairs, taking Brother Clarence with him and refusing to release his chokehold.

"Get him!" Seb shouts from under Brother's body.

I prop Anika against the closed door and run over, putting my hands on his burning hot head. Brother Clarence screams, body rattling as he tries to break free.

Seb grits his teeth struggling to hold him in place.

"Get out!" I bellow.

But I don't know what to do once the Echo leaves Brother Clarence, if he passes out like Anika. Who will say the spell? It's not like I know it.

Brother butts his head against Seb's snout, drawing blood. But Seb doesn't loosen his hold. He could probably bite the man easily, but not without killing him.

I need to do something to get the Echo out before Seb is forced to end him.

"Get out!" I shout again, afraid to close my eyes.

Brother meets my gaze and whispers, "Help me."

I don't know if he's talking to me or maybe praying to God. Either way, he closes his eyes.

"Get out!" I press my hands even harder to his skull.

The Echo leaps out and Brother's body goes limp.

The Echo looks down at Seb. *"Ah, you will make a great host,"* it says in a hardened and gnarled yore of a voice.

I can't let it get into Seb.

Not only would it likely kill us all, it would destroy Seb's life same as Anika's.

Same as it destroyed mine and Father's. Same as it murdered my mother.

I reach out and grab it, not even sure I can do what I want to, but knowing I need to try something.

I hear Brother Clarence in my head.

You are a Sin-Eater. Born to devour sins.

The Echo turns, surprised by my touch.

It looks like millions of flowing dark fibers, twisting and turning, undulating over one another, holding movement to maintain shape.

Its eyes meet mine.

"You cannot stop me. And I will not go back."

"No," I agree.

Memories flood my mind, from before I entered this realm — the sins I had taken. The Echoes I had already ingested and absorbed as a part of me.

It's why I see what I do. The Darkness has always been inside of me.

And it recognizes the Darkness in others. It's what I was made for.

I know what I must do now. It's the only way.

I throw my hands onto its head.

It lets out a high-pitched shriek that rattles the stairwell.

"What are you doing?"

"Get inside," I say.

Its eyes widen. It fears me. I can sense the terror, now that it knows what I am.

It lashes out, fist clenched into a claw, but it falls limp the moment it touches me.

I smile, squeezing its head tighter, my hands now glowing bright enough to blind me. "Get inside."

The Echo screams as its body starts to disintegrate into dark shreds of matter. I feel its fright and feed on its fear.

It all feels so natural.

You are a Sin-Eater. Born to devour sins.

I open my mouth, inhaling them, and it.

The Echo is inside me.

"Got you now, bitch." I smile.

I should be terrified, but there is no fear. I feel strangely complete, like some long-lost part of my soul has finally returned.

Seb is slow to stand. He's back in his human form, and naked, but he doesn't shy away or try to cover himself. His first impulse is to ask if I'm okay.

"It's inside of me," I tell him.

"What?"

Brother Clarence's voice is inside my head.

"It's okay. It's what you were born for."

His voice is frail. I look down and see he's unmoving.

I go to shake him.

No response.

Seb drops to one knee, trying to resuscitate him.

HA! The Echo laughs in my head. *HE'S DEAD.*

"I'm merely passing from one place to the next. You did good, my child. I'm proud of you."

What do I do about the Echo?

"Contain it. Don't let it win, and you'll be okay. Your father may be able to help you find someone to eliminate it. Ask him about The Night Society."

The what?

No response.

Brother Clarence is gone.

His absence is like the cold behind a closed door.

HE'S GONE. AND SOON YOUR FATHER WILL BE TOO. I WILL DESTROY EVERYTHING IN YOUR LIFE IF YOU REFUSE TO RELEASE ME!

The Echo's voice isn't old or leathery in my head. It's a

low baritone, almost comforting if it weren't trying to piss me off.

Shut up.

And, surprisingly, the voice is gone.

I actually shut it up.

I have control.

Seb looks up at me. "I'm sorry. He's gone."

He goes to check on Anika.

I drop down beside Brother Clarence, feeling a mix of sadness and anger. I'm mostly mad at myself. I ignored this man for so long, resented him for his role in helping Father use me to heal. I hadn't realized he never wanted to take part. That he'd risked his life bringing me to this realm. Brother Clarence saved me, and now he's gone before I could get to know him. Before I could learn more about our past, and what I really am. What he was.

What secrets was he holding?

I COULD TELL YOU. BUT ONLY IF YOU LET ME GO.

Shut up.

Seb, crouched over Anika, sighs with relief.

"She has a pulse, and I have smelling salts in the house if you want to get me some clothes."

I look back down at Brother Clarence, touch his head, and tell him how sorry I am.

Epilogue - Annika

Two days later

ANIKA IS SITTING in the same bar and the same booth in her restaurant where she met Delaney what feels like forever ago. She's been staring at the forged identification documents with the fake name, but her photos. Finally, she looks up at Delaney.

"You sure these will work?"

Delaney smiles. "My guy does great work. You'll be fine. Just stay out of this area until the heat dies down. Then look me up. Maybe we can figure out how to get your life back. Or, stay in Canada and enjoy this new one. Start over."

Anika's scared. What if the police manage to track her? She's responsible for many deaths, or at least the thing inside her was. Not that she can remember much of anything beyond what Delaney's told her. Most of it is a blur.

She voices her concerns to Delaney.

"Dusty assures me that the cops think it's a rival gang."

"And what about Jay's parents? What do they think?"

"I told them I had good reason to believe their son is dead, that Rufus more or less confessed it to several associates. Now that the gangster is gone, they'll have no reason to pursue it further."

"How did his mother take it?"

"Pretty bad. And she's upset that there isn't a body to bury. But it's better than not knowing. Living in the dark is always hardest. At least now she can find some closure."

"I feel awful for her. And Jay. I wish I could remember more of what happened."

"It's okay," Delaney says, putting her hand on Anika's. "Don't push it. Sometimes the mind blocks things out for a reason."

Anika nods. "How can I ever repay you?"

"By living your best life. And please, don't go back to pills."

Anika swears she never will, and this time she means it.

The constant sorrow and pain are strangely absent. She's scared of what's next, but it isn't the overwhelming terror that's been controlling most of her life.

"What happened to the monster?" she asks.

"It's gone. You're safe now. That's all that matters."

Anika wants to ask more, questions about the old black man and the werewolf, but something tells her it's best not to know. These people risked a lot and saved her, and that's all that really matters.

She hugs Del goodbye and leaves the bar.

～

ANIKA KNOCKS on Chelsea's door. She's already called and told her the lie Delaney arranged for her to tell, one that wouldn't leave her sister suspicious.

She supposedly witnessed some major crimes and has to enter witness protection. She can't be in touch for a while, but once able, Anika will make contact.

It's hard lying to Chelsea, but sometimes the truth is too much of a burden. She might blame herself for not knowing about the monster. She'd feel horrible. This way is easiest.

She opens the door and hugs Anika immediately. "I'm so sorry about everything."

"About what?"

"Not being there for you. For letting you go through all this alone while I was being a judgmental bitch."

"It's okay," Anika says, crying. "You were scared for me. I get it."

She wants to tell Chelsea that it wasn't her making all those horrible choices that got her hooked on drugs and dating a dealer. But Anika doesn't really know where she ended and the monster began.

But it's over now. Life is finally hers, maybe for the first time. She doesn't want to start this new life resenting Chelsea.

"You're my sister and you love me."

"I love you so damned much," Chelsea says, hugging her hard.

Anika feels that love, through a lens that no longer belongs to the monster.

And it feels like sunshine on her soul.

Epilogue - Delaney

I'm sitting at a table in the Morning Sun restaurant, waiting for Father to meet me for lunch.

I hope he's himself today.

We need to talk about Brother Clarence. I need to tell him I finally understand the sacrifices he made, and that I'm sorry for hating him.

I also have questions, but those will have to wait.

I retreat into my mind. A dark room with a bright red door. Locked with only one key. There's a small window in the door. It's been broken many times but it's not hard to imagine a new one to replace it.

I look inside at the Echo, sitting in a corner, sulking, drawing shadows around itself.

It looks at me, angry.

I open the door, not worried that it'll try to escape because the room is inside a larger room inside of yet another room inside so many more.

It cannot escape.

I enter and sit at a table as it materializes before me.

I create another chair.

"Ready to talk?"

LET ME GO.

"You know I can't do that. So why not make the best of this situation?"

I tap the table.

"Come on, talk to me. I want to know more about you."

It continues to sulk in the corner.

"Listen, I don't want you in me any more than you want to be here, but I'm not setting you free until I know you can't destroy other people's lives."

I CAN'T DESTROY ANYONE WHO ISN'T ALREADY CRAVING THE DARKNESS.

"The weak don't all want destruction. Those people need protection from you."

YOU THINK KEEPING ME IN HERE IS SAVING THE WORLD? DO YOU KNOW HOW MANY MORE OF ME THERE ARE? HOW MANY THE ANCIENT HAS BROUGHT OVER? HOW MANY YOU ARE RESPONSIBLE FOR BRINGING HERE?

"What do you mean I'm responsible?"

It laughs in the corner, then in a sing-song voice it says, *I KNOW SOMETHING YOU DON'T KNOW.*

"What?"

THIS IS ALL BECAUSE BROTHER CLARENCE BROUGHT YOU HERE. HE OPENED THE PORTAL AND GAVE US OUR DOORWAY. SO, THANK YOU, DELANEY. WHEN BEZ KYEHVE WAS IN YOU AND YOUR FATHER, HE BROUGHT MORE OVER. SOOOOOO MANY MORE OF US THAN YOU EVEN KNOW. DO YOU PLAN TO TRAP US ALL IN HERE?

The Echo laughs.

I get up and leave, slamming the door behind me.

I open my eyes.

Father's nurse is wheeling him to my table. I can't tell if he's himself.

I need him to be here. I need to tell him I'm sorry. I need to tell him I love him. I need to open myself up in a way I've always been afraid to. If I'm going to get through this, I need to change. Make amends before my father is no longer with me.

With Brother Clarence gone, he's the only person in my life who knows me. And I've kept him at such a distance for too long.

After my amends, I'll figure out what to do about this Echo inside me. Can it be returned to the In-Between or am I stuck with it forever? I need to find out if something can be done about the others out there, possessing people and doing God knows what.

And I need to know what the hell The Night Society is.

A new nurse I don't recognize smiles at me. "Here's your daughter, Mr. Jennings."

He pats her hand and says, "Thank you."

She leaves us.

I meet Father's eye, tell him I'm sorry, then stand to hug him. From within our embrace I say, "I know you protected me from what I did. I'm sorry … and I love you."

Father hugs me back.

And in that hug, I see … nothing.

His memories are static.

I pull away.

Tears are dotting his cheeks. "Do I know you?"

"It's me, Delaney."

Father stares at me blankly. "I'm sorry, ma'am. I … I'm not feeling myself."

He calls for the nurse.

The Echo inside me laughs.

HE'S GONE. I CAN GO INSIDE HIM, MAYBE BRING HIM BACK IF YOU WANT.

I get up and leave, weeping as I go.

This isn't over. I'm not giving up. I'll keep coming back until he returns. I'll never give up on my father. Or on figuring this out. There has to be something I can do to find others infected with the Echoes and rid the world of these monsters.

Maybe it's time to stop seeing my gift as a curse, as a burden to bear alone.

Maybe it's time to stop closing myself off from those who want to be in my life.

Maybe I should let them help me with this battle.

Except I know in my soul there's no *maybe* about it.

Noella's only happiness comes in her dreams of a world where her father is alive and a mysterious stranger protects her from the monsters of her nightmares. Then those monsters walk into her waking life. Is Noella losing her mind, or is she linked to a hidden word, destined to be normal ForNevermore?

GET FORNEVERMORE

A Quick Favor...

If you enjoyed this book, please take a moment to write a short review on your favorite online bookstore so other readers can enjoy it, too.

Thanks so much!
Sean & Dave

About the Authors

Sean Platt is an entrepreneur and founder of Sterling & Stone, where he makes stories with his partners, Johnny B. Truant, and David W. Wright, and a family of storytellers.

Sean is the bestselling author of over 10 million words' worth of books, including the Yesterday's Gone and Invasion series. Sean is also co-author of the indie publishing cornerstone, Write. Publish. Repeat. and co-host of the Story Studio Podcast.

Originally from Long Beach, California, Sean now lives in Austin, Texas with his wife and two children. He has more than his share of nose.

~

David W. Wright is the co-author of edge-of-your seat thrillers including the best-selling post-apocalyptic series *Yesterday's Gone,* the paranoid sci-fi *WhiteSpace* series, and the vigilante series, *No Justice,* as well as standalone thrillers *12,* and *Crash* which was recently optioned for a movie.

David is an accomplished, though intermittent, cartoonist who lives in [LOCATION REDACTED] with his wife and son [NAMES REDACTED.]

He is not at all paranoid.

He is "the grumpy one" on the *The Story Studio Podcast* with fellow Sterling and Stone founders, Sean Platt and Johnny B. Truant.

David writes about books, TV shows, movies, and

video games he enjoys; his struggles with anxiety and OCD; writing; and posts the occasional drawing at his personal blog at davidwwright.com

You can email him at david@sterlingandstone.net

We swear, he almost never bites. Unless you feed him after midnight.

For a full list of his most recent books visit sterlingandstone.net.

Also By Sean Platt

The Dead World Series

Dead Zero

Dead City

Dead Nation

Dead Planet

Empty Nest

The Beam Series

The Beam Season One

The Beam Season Two

The Beam Season Three

Robot Proletariat Series

En3my

Robot Proletariat

The Infinite Loop

The Hard Reset

Cascade Failure

Reboot

The Tomorrow Gene Series

Null Identity

The Tomorrow Gene

The Tomorrow Clone

The Eden Experiment

Karma Police Series

Jumper

Karma Police

The Collectors

Deviant

The Fall

Homecoming

Yesterday's Gone

October's Gone

Yesterday's Gone Season One

Yesterday's Gone Season Two

Yesterday's Gone Season Three

Yesterday's Gone Season Four

Yesterday's Gone Season Five

Yesterday's Gone Season Six

Tomorrow's Gone

Tomorrow's Gone Season One

Tomorrow's Gone Season Two

Tomorrow's Gone Season Three

Available Darkness

Darkness Itself

Available Darkness Book One

Available Darkness Book Two

Available Darkness Book Three

WhiteSpace

WhiteSpace Season One

WhiteSpace Season Two

WhiteSpace Season Three

Stand Alone Novels

Burnout

The Island

Crash

Emily's List

Pattern Black

Devil May Care

Also By David W. Wright

ForNevermore

ForNevermore Season One

ForNevermore Season Two

ForNevermore Season Three

Hidden Justice

Hidden Justice

Hidden Honor

Hidden Shame

Hidden Virtue

No Justice

No Justice

No Escape

No Hope

No Return

No Stopping

No Fear

Karma Police

Jumper

Karma Police

The Collectors

Deviant

The Fall

Homecoming

Yesterday's Gone

October's Gone

Yesterday's Gone Season One

Yesterday's Gone Season Two

Yesterday's Gone Season Three

Yesterday's Gone Season Four

Yesterday's Gone Season Five

Yesterday's Gone Season Six

Tomorrow's Gone

Tomorrow's Gone Season One

Tomorrow's Gone Season Two

Tomorrow's Gone Season Three

Available Darkness

Darkness Itself

Available Darkness Book One

Available Darkness Book Two

Available Darkness Book Three

WhiteSpace

WhiteSpace Season One

WhiteSpace Season Two

WhiteSpace Season Three

Stand Alone Novels

12

Crash
Emily's List
Threshold
The Secret Within